TEMPTATION

Sydney Campbell

ISBN: 978-1-7774505-2-6

Cover design by abu-chan

For all of you who believed I could pull this off.

Other books by Sydney Campbell:

Allie Styles Romance Series:
Temptation (Book 1)
Deception (Book 2)
Reckonings (Book 3)
Beginnings (Book 4)

Courtyard Tales of Contemporary Romance
Reawakening
Redemption
Reckless

CHAPTER ONE

It was our fifth date, which I suppose is why Pete thought it would be okay to take my hand as we made our way across the crowded cobblestone street in search of his friends. Five meticulously planned dates, during which he'd upped his courting game each time. There was zero chemistry between us, but it seemed he hadn't figured that out yet.

I knew this wasn't going anywhere. Pete was my rebound. At 31, I was six months out of a long-term relationship that had broken my heart, and I needed someone safe and comforting. He was definitely that. I knew I'd have to break it off with him eventually, but I was still semi-enjoying the idea of him.

It was a beautiful night; the sky clear and

filled with stars – a rare sight in the city. We passed bar after bar on the popular Montreal downtown strip. Music blared from open doorways as people spilled out into the street, laughing, touching, kissing—lips and inhibitions loosened by drink.

"There they are," Pete said, pulling my hand while I resisted the urge to jerk it away. He led me to an outdoor table where I recognized three of the four guys sitting there, but the last one... him I'd never seen before.

He had a medium build, with dark curly hair. He stood when he saw me approach, like some throwback to the fifties when chivalry was alive and well. He was tall, over six feet, and he wore jeans and an old Led Zeppelin concert shirt. He squared his shoulders and I couldn't help but notice the muscle ripple underneath that shirt. I walked towards him, pulled as if by some magnetic force. He had sea-green eyes... When they locked with mine, I knew I was in trouble.

"Hey," he said. "Matt."

"Hi," I said, putting out my hand. "Allie."

He took my hand and everything inside me simultaneously froze and caught fire. He quickly let go and motioned to the empty chair behind me. We both sat, and he eyed me carefully. The ice vanished; I was pure fire. He had a small scar over his left eye, and I wanted nothing more than to reach over and touch it. Pete looked over with a smile, squeezed my knee and turned to chat with his friend, Dave. *Shit.*

"Allie," Matt said. "That's short for..."

"Allison, yes. But it's been Allie for as long as I can remember."

He glanced at my knee, where Pete's hand still rested.

"Been seeing Pete long?" Matt asked, with a mischievous edge to his voice.

"No," I said casually. "Fifth date, maybe?"

He nodded towards my knee and whispered, "Pretty handsy, no?"

I laughed, shifting position. Pete's hand fell from my leg. I looked Matt straight in the eye.

"Better?"

Matt raised his eyebrows and tipped back his beer bottle, emptying the contents into his mouth. The heat burned through my body as he studied my face.

"How'd you meet?" he asked.

"At a bar. Much like this one. With many of the same people. But you weren't there."

Matt smiled and was about to respond when we were interrupted by the waiter, bringing over drinks I hadn't noticed Pete order. He handed me a glass and I smiled in thanks, taking a sip. Vodka and soda. Five dates and the guy couldn't remember I drank gin and tonic. He turned back to Dave to resume his sports talk. I stared at my glass.

"Not your drink?" Matt asked.

"How'd you know?" I said, laughing.

"I've known Pete a long time."

"Wrong glass for the drink, too."

"Are you a bartender?"

"Food critic. But you're changing the subject. Why haven't we met before?"

"Right. I just got back from six months abroad. On a work contract."

I nodded, heart racing as I stared into those green eyes. I couldn't pull my gaze away. Finally, he tilted his head, raised his eyebrows, and smiled in a way that pierced me to the core. He had a gleam in his eye as he leaned in towards me.

"You two serious?"

"Pete and I? No," I said, wondering why I was revealing this to one of Pete's friends. But I had lost any semblance of control over the conversation the moment I sat down at the table. I took a sip of my drink.

"Have you slept with him?"

"Excuse me?" I asked, almost spitting out my not-gin-and-tonic.

"Complicates things if you have," he mused

aloud. "Well, it complicates them even more."

"What makes you think you've even got a shot?" I asked, trying for an indignant tone.

He just looked at me. Every once in a while he rubbed the scar over his eye, the only evidence of self-consciousness he displayed. I wanted to touch it.

I looked over guiltily at Pete, still engrossed in conversation. He must've felt my glance because he reached over absently to rub my arm. I looked back at Matt.

"You felt it, too. When I took your hand," he said.

"I felt it."

He pulled his chair in a little closer, his leg brushing up against my thigh. I could smell him. Some familiar hair product with the faint hint of soap beneath it mixed with his own scent. I could barely swallow. I blushed. He tucked a stray lock of hair behind my ear, and I trembled slightly. There was no denying it. The chemistry was palpable.

"I slept with him," I whispered, so quietly it was almost inaudible.

"Shit," he said, a little too loudly.

"What's the matter?" Pete asked, turning his attention to us. "Is there a problem?"

Matt just smiled at him.

"Don't worry," he said. "We'll work it out."

I cleared my throat, suddenly uncomfortable. How on earth did I get myself into this situation? I turned to Pete.

"Actually," I said, "I'm not feeling that well. I'm a bit… warm."

I heard Matt chuckle under his breath. Dave peered around Pete and gave us both a quizzical glance.

"Do you think you could take me home?" I asked.

Pete looked back at his buddies with a moment of regret before turning back to me.

"Sure. Of course. Let's go."

He stood up and held out a hand to me. I pretended not to see it, as I bent down in search of my purse. I grabbed my bag, feeling the heat spread across my face, and stood up. I smiled at Pete and turned to say goodbye to his friends. As we started away, Matt called out, "Hey, Pete. Think I could get a ride?"

"Dude. Of course. Come on."

I froze. *How dare he?* competed heavily with *He wants me!*, leaving me in a state of complete paralysis. Pete grabbed my hand and started walking, Matt following a few paces behind. I was numb but decided to let him hold my hand, being a little unsteady on my feet. I could feel Matt's eyes boring holes through my back.

When we got to the car, Matt came up beside me.

"Want the front?" I asked him.

"Don't be silly. You take it. Girlfriend privileges."

Pete grinned like an idiot and unlocked the doors.

"This is a fifth date," I said. "A little early for labels. But thanks for the seat."

I slid into the car, determined to remain silent for the duration of the ride. As I strapped on my seatbelt, Pete pulled away from the curb and drove slowly down the busy street. He fiddled with the radio as he navigated his way towards the highway.

"Where you headed?" he asked Matt.

"Drop me at the apartment," Matt said. "I'll do some painting."

I turned in my seat to face him.

"The apartment?" I said, bewildered.

"Yeah, I told you," Pete said. "Matt is the third roommate I'm moving in with."

I stared at Matt, mouth agape. He grinned, shrugged, and raised his eyebrows. *Complicated*, he mouthed. I turned back to face the front and closed my eyes. Resting my head against the back of my seat, it struck me.

"You're Goldberg," I said.

"At your service," he replied.

CHAPTER TWO

We drove in silence for a while, listening to some Top 40 station on the radio. Pete's taste in music sucked. My mind raced, trying to make sense of all this information. *Fuck.* Maybe if they had just been acquaintances. But roommates? I'd gone low before, but never that low.

"You can drop Allie first, if that's easier," Matt said, completely out of the blue.

I knew exactly what he was thinking.

"Nah," Pete answered.

A few minutes later, we pulled up outside a small, three-floor apartment building on a tree-lined street. It was very pretty, in a nice part of town. I understood why it took three of them to afford it. It put my one-bedroom on the busy corner of a shitty area to shame.

"That's ours," Pete said, pointing towards the first-floor bay window. I smiled.

"Looks great," I said. "When do you guys move in?"

"In two weeks," Pete answered. "We want to finish stripping and painting first."

Matt unstrapped his seat belt and opened the door.

"Invite her in," he said.

"Great idea!" Pete smiled and unstrapped his own seatbelt.

I looked at him for a moment, about to plead out with a headache, but I bit my tongue. Butterflies erupted in my stomach. *This is a bad move*, I thought to myself. But I figured I'd just stay a few minutes. No harm, no foul.

I unhooked my own belt and opened the door. As I stepped onto the sidewalk, I tried to keep my eyes down, but I caught a quick glimpse of Matt's triumphant grin. Suddenly, I grew dizzy. I put my hand out on the roof of the car to steady myself and felt Matt's strong hand grip my elbow.

"You okay?" he asked, concerned.

Pete was by his side in a flash, taking my other arm. Matt didn't let go, and I took a moment to marvel at the different sensations I experienced, on my right and left side. The arm in Matt's possession was on fire. The one in Pete's was not.

"I'm fine," I insisted. "Just a headache. I told you. Let's go in."

Matt finally withdrew his hand, leaving me in Pete's care. We climbed the few steps to the front door and entered the front hallway. It was old-fashioned, but clean and warm. There were a few upholstered chairs in the front lobby area, which was tiny with cream-coloured walls. Through that space was the hall that held two apartment doors and the staircase. There was no elevator. It was quiet compared to my building.

Pete fiddled with the key while Matt leaned back against the wall, openly taking me in from head to toe. I tilted my head, giving him my best *Are you fucking kidding me?* stare. Then he smiled, and I couldn't help but smile back.

"Where do you live?" he asked.

"Not far," I answered.

I was determined to give nothing else away. This couldn't go anywhere, and I wasn't going to encourage him. Pete finally got the door open and I followed him into the apartment. Matt made a show of letting me go first.

Pete took me around, showing me the living room, dining room, and kitchen. The space was well laid out, with each room flowing into the other. There was only a short hallway between the dining room and the kitchen, which contained three doors, leading to two bedrooms and a bathroom. Matt was setting up a ladder in the kitchen and opening paint cans.

"Aren't there three of you?" I asked.

"Yes," Pete answered. He pointed towards the first bedroom and said, "Mine." He then pointed to the second bedroom and said, "Dave's." I craned my neck to get a glimpse of Matt in the kitchen.

"What about him?" I asked.

Pete laughed, took me by the hand and led me into the kitchen. It was large, with enough space for a table and chairs. They'd already started painting the room a bright yellow. A lazy boy chair was set up in the corner.

"Don't tell me you sleep there," I said, mortified.

They both laughed. Matt put down the paint brush and opened a door off to the side of the room. I pushed past the ladder and peered in. It was an eight by eight-foot space with a tiny window up near the ceiling.

"You're going to live in the pantry?" I asked.

"No, I'm going to sleep in the pantry," Matt said.

Pete laughed. "He doesn't need a lot of

space. He's— "

Matt interrupted him. "...all alone. It's plenty of room."

He gave me that smile that made me blush. The headache was setting in for real now. I turned to find Pete looking at Matt with a quizzical expression on his face. I filed that away for later.

"Can you take me home?" I asked him.

He broke his gaze from Matt and looked at me, giving me a salute. I suppressed the urge to roll my eyes.

"Of course. Let's go."

I turned to leave and felt Matt's hand on my arm. I turned quickly, anxious to break contact.

"Yes?" I said.

"I just wanted to say goodbye," he said, smiling. "It was nice meeting you."

Pete took my hand and led me out of the apartment. I was silent the entire drive home, while he rattled on about the upcoming football season. I had zero interest in sports. I had even less interest in Pete at this point. *What the fuck was I going to do?* Clearly, there was nothing I could do. I would break up with Pete and never see either of them again. Done.

A part of me-a *miniscule* part of me-debated the whole breaking up with Pete thing. Yes, he was starting to make my skin crawl. But in two weeks, he was moving in with Matt. I knew it was wrong. It was asking for trouble. But sometimes a little trouble… No. I wasn't going there.

I was irrationally angry with myself, feeling like I'd missed out on the chance for the rebound relationship of a lifetime – hot guy, hot sex, no strings. After all the grieving I'd done for Josh, I deserved that much. No doubt Josh had had a string of women by this time. Not that he was that type. *Oh, Josh.*

I was so lost in thought I hadn't even noticed Pete had pulled up outside my building and turned off the ignition. Panic gripped me. He went to open his door and I braced myself. *It's okay. He can walk you to the door.* I unhooked my seat belt and opened the door before he could do it for me. It was meant to be chivalrous, but at this point, anything he did was bound to irritate me.

We walked up the steps and stopped at the landing. He waited while I fished around in my purse for my keys. I pulled them out and looked up at him. He just stood there, waiting.

"Listen," I said. "I've got a really bad headache."

Ironically enough, I was no longer lying. Still, he looked crushed.

"Okay," he said.

He turned to go, then turned back and leaned in for a kiss. The moment his lips touched mine I knew I couldn't do it. I pulled back.

"My head, Pete..." I said.

He nodded, turned, and went down the steps.

CHAPTER THREE

I climbed the two flights of stairs to my apartment and worked the key in the lock. I opened the door, and Loki, my 70-lb black mutt, immediately came up to greet me. I knelt to pet her, looking around for her leash.

"Want to go for a walk?" I asked.

She ran in the opposite direction and jumped on the couch. *Okay*, I thought. My neighbour must have walked her earlier. I put down my bag. Unlike Pete, my apartment was small. But it was well thought out. The bedroom was immediately off to the left and a short hallway led to a bathroom. Then it opened into the living room, which had a door leading to the kitchen. All three rooms were large, given the size of the apartment. *Plenty of room*, I thought. *After all, I'm all alone.*

I walked into the kitchen and opened the cupboard over the sink, taking out a small wooden box, and carried it to the kitchen table. I'd inherited the table from my grandmother – meaning I took it from her apartment when she passed away. It was far from antique. Very Ikea-style and bought in the last ten years. But it suited my needs and she was great in the kitchen, so I figured it had good karma.

I sat down, opened the box, and got to work rolling a joint. When I was done, I grabbed an ashtray and headed for the living room.

The living room was oddly shaped, with no two walls of equal length. The couch was set against the back wall, along a row of windows. I had a smaller love seat on the right, with a coffee table accessible to both. Three of the walls were painted white, and the fourth a deep red. I'd been there two years and the apartment looked lived in – various prints hanging, trinkets on the mantle. I settled onto the couch and propped my feet up on the table as I lit my joint. I picked up the remote, twirled it in my fingers for a few minutes, then put it down.

I knew where he was. I knew he was alone. I could go back there. What would he do? What would even happen? He'd been pretty forward all night – what would he do if he had me alone... and willing? I slid down a little, running my hand up my thigh, remembering the fireworks and butterflies from earlier. I closed my eyes and I could smell him, feel the heat of his leg beside mine.

What would he do if he opened the door and there I was? My hand rested above my lower belly, feeling the ache beneath my jeans. I undid the button and pulled down the zipper.

He'd probably just stand there for a moment, in shock. Or would he be cocky, having known I'd come back? Both fantasies were equally tempting. I slid my hand into my underwear, feeling how ready I was, how close I was just thinking about him. My breath came quicker, and I put the joint down in the ashtray, sliding further down on the couch.

I'd reach out and touch the scar over his eye, and he'd pull me inside the apartment, needing nothing more in the way of invitation. Pushing me up against the wall, he'd reach behind me, take my hair, and twist it up behind my head as he leaned in for a kiss. And he'd know how to kiss.

He'd break away, briefly, to look me in the eye and smile. Definitely cocky. Then he'd move back in again, kissing my mouth, my cheek, my neck, as he moved his way down. He'd take a step back, unwrapping my arms from his neck and looking me over from head to toe in that way that made me shiver. I arched my back.

He'd reach out and carefully unbutton each button on my shirt, so slowly it felt like I would scream. Pushing the shirt aside, he'd undo the clasp on my bra, between my breasts. He'd trail his fingers lightly across my skin. I could feel it tingle in his wake, the nerve endings firing under his touch. He'd cup my breast, lean in, and... Waves washed over me as my orgasm swept through my body, forcing me to clutch the blanket on the couch next to me with my free hand. The sensation was so overpowering I didn't want to stop, and I kept picturing him, rubbing my nipple with his thumb, leaning in to take it into his mouth... The second wave came over more violently than the first and I actually cried out, shocking both myself and the dog, who leapt off the couch and ran for the bedroom.

I laughed, shook myself out of my reverie and picked up the joint.

CHAPTER FOUR

I woke up the next day, still fully dressed on the couch, with total cotton mouth. Loki was whining by the door, so I rolled off the couch, grabbed my shoes and her leash and out we went.

We walked out the front door and turned on to the quieter side street. I lived in a pretty seedy part of town, but the rent was cheap, and Loki was a good guard dog. It was still relatively early, before eleven o'clock, and the streets were quiet. As I watched Loki sniff the grass and traces of urine left behind by previous dogs, I thought about my behaviour the night before. My phone rang.

"Allie?" Pete said. "Just checking to make

sure you're okay."

"I'm fine, Pete. Thanks," I said. "Listen, I'm just walking the dog…"

"Yeah, sure, no problem," he said. "Listen, I was wondering if you'd want to come help paint the apartment tonight. You don't have to paint, maybe just keep me company. I'll pick up a bottle of wine."

I thought about it for a moment. I could use the opportunity to break up with him. Over a bottle of wine. It would be civilized.

"Sure," I said. "I'll be there at 8."

Loki and I rounded the corner and headed back up to the apartment. After a quick shower and some fresh clothing, I checked my reflection in the mirror. My hair fell just below my shoulders, the curls dragging, indicating it was time for a cut. I momentarily considered the brown locks, wondering if I should start colouring my hair. Maybe some highlights? I stepped back, taking in the full picture. Despite the recent lack of exercise and over-indulgence in junk food, the body was still looking good.

I looked at the time and ran out the front door to meet Lynn, my best friend and today's lunch companion. As feared, she was sitting at a table on the terrace with an irate expression on her face.

"I'm so sorry," I said, as I slid into the seat

across from her. "I know I'm late. Traffic was horrible. But you can't be mad at me. I'm paying for lunch."

"Humph," she replied, glaring at me, all stern-faced, before breaking into a smile. She shook her head. "It's lucky you're paying."

I laughed and picked up the menu, looking around. It was a cute restaurant, brand new in the neighbourhood. The chef was from Chicago, relocating to Montreal after a messy divorce with his wife. The décor, even outdoors, was very masculine. Lots of wood and polished brass. Through the terrace doors I could see the bar, furnished much the same way. I looked back at Lynn, who was studying me quizzically.

"Late night?" she asked. "How was it?"

I rolled my eyes and perused the menu.

"Order at least two appetizers," I said. "And two mains."

"God, I love going out for lunch with you."

The waiter came by and took our orders and our menus. He returned a few moments later with our drinks, and Lynn sat silently, waiting.

"So? What happened?" she asked.

"It was nothing. Really. I had a headache. Cut the night short."

"Thank the Lord," she said. "I have no idea what you see in that guy. Eager like a puppy, bouncing around all over the place. What is it with him?"

"I don't know. He's what I thought I should want, I guess. Someone safe and eager to commit – the opposite of Josh. I know I have to break it off. I plan on doing it tonight. He invited me over to paint the new apartment."

Lynn rolled her eyes.

"Well, there's a tempting offer."

I smiled, tracing my finger along my thigh under the table. I wondered how Matt got the scar. Childhood accident? Snowboarding as a teen? Though he didn't look the snowboarding type. Thank god. Not that it mattered, even. Nothing could ever happen.

Shit. How did I get here? Maybe he got the scar in a fight. I resolved that if I did see him again, I'd ask. My fingers ached to touch it, to trace its line over the corner of his eyebrow. Lightly. Ever so lightly. Then he'd take my hand away, and holding it in his, kiss my fingertips – one by one.

"ALLIE!" Lynn hissed. "Where are you?"

I looked at her, momentarily startled, my thumb still making small circles on my leg. I shook my head to clear it and laughed.

"Off in the clouds, I guess," I said.

"I want to know *exactly* what you were just thinking about. Spill it."

As if sent by the angels themselves, the waiter appeared with our appetizers. He looked at the two of us, and at the amount of food he was carrying, and almost imperceptibly shrugged to himself. I laughed inwardly. The life of a food critic – everyone just thinking I'm a pig.

I looked over the offering, picked up my fork and started sampling.

"Don't fill up," I warned.

"You're changing the subject."

"I was thinking about last night."

"A night with Pete leads to daydreaming on an epic scale?"

Lynn looked at me with her trademark skeptical expression.

"Fine. Never mind. You'll tell me when you're ready. You always do. Fifteen years I've known you, nothing changes."

We ate silently for a while, occasionally trading notes on a dish.

"When's the review due?" she asked.

"In the morning. And I was serious – don't fill up. I hear they have excellent desserts."

"God, I love going to lunch with you."

CHAPTER FIVE

That night, I pulled on some old sweats and a T-shirt, tied my hair up in a ponytail and drove over to Pete's new apartment. I figured it might be easier on him if I didn't look hot when I broke it off.

I rang his apartment and he buzzed me in. He had the biggest, goofiest grin on his face when he saw me. He opened the door wide and swept me into the apartment, planting a kiss on my mouth.

"I'm so happy you came," he said.

I just smiled and followed him into the apartment, realizing I'd made a mistake. I should've done this over the phone. What if he had some big romantic evening planned? I scanned the rooms, looking for signs of a picnic basket or candles. Nothing. Okay.

He led me into the living room, which was covered in drop clothes and open paint cans. "You want to help, or do you want to watch?" he asked, grinning.

"Listen, Pete..."

He grabbed a brush and crossed the room towards me in two strides. He placed the brush in my hands.

"I really think we should talk..."

"More painting, less talking."

He got back to work. I sighed and lifted my hand to stare at the brush. I looked around and saw a ladder set up against the wall to reach the trim. Some things just take a woman's touch. Or at least someone who can keep still for five minutes.

He paused his work to turn on some music and we painted in relative silence for a few moments. I was staring up at the ceiling, trying to figure out how to break the news to him, when the front door opened and Dave called out, "We got the beer!"

We?

"Shit," Pete said. "I told you wine."

"I got beer," Dave said.

"Who the fuck drinks wine anyway?" Matt asked, entering the apartment. He stopped short when he saw me on the step ladder, and I simultaneously froze and lost my balance. I tried to steady myself against the wall, but it was covered in wet paint and as my hand slipped, I went backwards off the ladder.

Matt bounded across the room and caught me just as I fell. Dave slowly put down the case of beer he was carrying while Pete stood there, paint brush in hand, looking like a complete idiot. I looked up at Matt, who was looking at me with worry in his eyes.

"You okay?" he asked.

I nodded slowly, and it felt like time stopped and everything around us melted away as I stood there, gathered up in his arms, staring into his eyes. My heart was beating so fast I couldn't hear the conversation going on around me. Suddenly Pete was there beside Matt, looking at me and reaching out to take my hand. Matt squeezed me a little tighter before letting go, surrendering me to Pete's care.

I didn't want Pete's care. I wanted to be back in Matt's arms.

"Maybe a beer?" I said.

Pete nodded and Dave tossed him a bottle. Pete opened it and handed it to me. I sat down on the floor and took a long drink.

"What happened there?" Pete asked.

"I was just surprised when Dave came in,

that's all," I said. "I thought it was just the two of us tonight. He caught me off guard."

"Oh," Pete said, reconsidering. "It was Matt's idea to invite you, actually. I didn't think you'd be into it. Would you rather go elsewhere?"

I hesitated. I knew walking out the door that minute was the best thing I could do for all three of us. But I also knew that, more than anything, I wanted to stay. *It was Matt's idea.* The words had set a thousand butterflies loose in my stomach. He wanted to spend time with me.

"No," I said. "It's okay. Let's paint."

Matt had been standing off to the side this whole time, watching the exchange with great interest. He wore a slight grin, which didn't go unnoticed by Dave, who consequently rolled his eyes to the ceiling.

"A situation is what we've got here," Dave muttered as he made his way to the kitchen with the case of beer.

My phone rang, and I looked down to see the number. Lynn. I smiled at Pete and answered. She was talking a mile a minute. I put my hand over the phone and said to Pete, "I'll be right back."

I left the apartment and sat down in one of the lobby armchairs.

"Slow down," I said. "Tell me what's going on."

Apparently, Lynn had had some horrible blind date experience and just needed to let off some steam. I listened sympathetically for a while, then we said good night. When I got up to go back into the apartment, I saw Matt leaning against the doorframe.

"Problem?" he asked.

"I don't know. Is there?"

He laughed.

"This was your idea? What were you thinking?" I asked.

"He wasn't supposed to tell you that," he said, but looked me straight in the eye as he said it.

My heart stopped. I opened my mouth slightly, just to breathe a little easier. I took a few steps, closing the distance between us. The door to the apartment was open, and I didn't want to be overheard.

"Nothing is going to happen with us," I said. "Pete is your roommate. I don't even know what you're thinking. You have to *live* with him. Why would you want to do this?"

Matt shrugged. I rolled my eyes and pushed past him, back into the apartment.

"There you are!" Pete said. "Everything okay?"

"Yeah, everything's fine," I said.

I picked up my brush, but rather than climb back up the ladder, I focused on the trim around the windows. The guys talked sports and joked around with each other while they worked. I was mostly quiet, having no interest in sports. I peered over at Matt and watched the muscles of his arm flex as he made long strokes with his paint brush. His shoulders were magnificent, broad, and thick. He turned suddenly and caught my eye. I gripped my brush tighter and turned back to my trim. Once again, I'd found myself in an impossible situation.

"So, Allie, how's work going? Eat anywhere good lately?" Dave asked.

Dave and I knew each other before Pete entered the picture. We had common friends, and I had bumped into him that night at the bar when I met Pete. Or rather when Dave introduced me to Pete. *Fuck.* Why hadn't Matt just been there that night? This whole situation could've been avoided.

"Yeah," I said. "There are some great new spots opening up. And Mythos just got a new chef who's fantastic."

"How come you never take me out to eat?" Pete said.

I knew this was coming, and I was prepared.

"I don't want to mix work and play," I said. "I tend to eat with only a few select people. It's easier that way for me to keep balance in my life."

"Hmm… I guess." Pete said.

He turned back to his roller and started painting again. Matt walked over to open a fresh can of paint and looked at what I was doing.

"You missed a spot," he said, casually.

"Where?" I asked, looking the trim up and down.

He walked over behind me and pointed over my shoulder.

"Right there."

I looked again. Saw nothing. I turned and looked at him. He rolled his eyes, took my hand in his and together we painted over an imaginary missed spot on the wall. He was so close I could feel his breath in my ear, smell that heady, familiar scent that enveloped him. Every fiber of my being wanted to turn and kiss him. I pulled my hand away.

"Matt, dude, can I see you in the kitchen for a moment? I want to talk curtains," Dave said.

He punched Matt on the shoulder and stood there, waiting for his friend to follow him into the kitchen. The two guys took off down the hall. I looked over at Pete.

"Are you fucking nuts?" Dave hissed at Matt.

Shit.

"Hey," I said to Pete. "Can I talk to you for a moment? In private?"

"No one's here," he said, looking around.

"Let's go in your room," I said.

His face lit up and I instantly regretted the suggestion. He dropped his roller, took my hand, and led me to his bedroom. There was nothing in there save a few chairs. Thank goodness no bed yet. He closed the door behind him and came towards me. I sat down abruptly.

"Listen, Pete, I don't think this is going to work out."

He stopped short. It was almost comical. For a moment I thought he was going to topple over, head-first.

"What? I don't get it."

"There's nothing really for you to understand. I'm just not ready to be dating someone. You know I was in a long relationship, and I thought I was ready, but I'm just not."

"So? Let's keep going out. I'm not pressuring you into anything serious. We're having fun."

I stopped, wondering how to handle this.

"Listen, Pete. I think, and I may be wrong, but I think you like me a little more than I like you. And I don't want to hurt you. I don't want to lead you on. You know what I mean?"

He snorted.

"You might have thought of that before you slept with me."

I sighed. The truth was, I slept with him because I didn't want him going down on me. The first time we fooled around he displayed a sure manner combined with a complete lack of skill. He was a decent kisser, but it was clear he had zero knowledge of the female anatomy, and I dreaded the kind of shitshow he'd put on down there. Sex seemed easier. Apparently, I was wrong.

"Look," I said. "I'm sorry. I really am. But this is where I am right now."

He went from stunned, to angry, back to stunned before he put out a hand to stop me.

"Okay," he said. "Enough."

I looked at him with more than a little sympathy and guilt.

"I think maybe I should go," I said.

"Yeah. I think that would be a good idea."

CHAPTER SIX

I stepped out the front door of the building and took in a deep breath of the cool night air. *What a relief,* I thought. I should've broken up with him a few dates back, and the added stress of having Matt in the picture was too much for me to deal with. I had just eliminated two birds with one stone. I practically skipped down the steps and turned up the sidewalk.

I was halfway down the block when I heard footsteps coming up fast behind me. I instinctively pulled my right hand, but there was no leash, and no dog to draw closer. *Probably just Pete, making a last-ditch effort,* I thought. I stopped and turned, prepared to talk him down. It was Matt.

"Oh," I said.

"You okay?" he asked, coming to a stop before me.

"Of course I'm okay. What are you doing here? Are you fucking nuts?"

"Dave asked me the same question," he laughed. "Don't worry. Pete's locked in his room, trying to decide between outrage and heartbreak. Whatever he decides, it'll be dramatic."

"Sorry to leave you with that," I said, turning to continue towards my car.

"I'll walk you," he said, falling into step beside me. "Where are you parked?"

"Around the block."

"Good," he said, smiling that smile that made my insides quiver.

We walked in silence, not really knowing what to say to each other. It wasn't awkward, though. It was easy.

"I'm right up there," I said, pointing towards my car.

"I want to kiss you," he said suddenly, sending my mind reeling. "But I can't. That's my buddy in there. And right now, he's pretty miserable. Over you. So I really I can't."

I stopped walking when we reach the car and I turned towards him. I stared at the small scar over his eye, again wanting to reach out and touch it. Bar fight? Jealous ex-girlfriend? I tilted my head and studied his face.

"Of course you can't. It would be wrong. It doesn't matter that I've broken up with Pete. Nothing can ever happen with us. The sooner you accept that, the better," I said.

I got into my car and drove away.

CHAPTER SEVEN

I spent the next seven days keeping busy with work and Loki. Five reviews in one week was more than my waistline could bear, so I made a point of heading to the gym, too, something I detested under normal circumstances. Now, however, it was a welcome distraction.

I'd broken up with Pete and eliminated any possibility of seeing Matt again. Now I just needed to move on.

"We're going out tonight," Lynn said over the phone.

"Dinner?" I asked, hopefully.

"Drinking. I'll pick you up in an hour."

I got myself ready for a night out. Just because I couldn't have Matt, it didn't mean I couldn't have anyone. Maybe some fresh blood would take my mind off things. I smoked a joint while getting dressed, picking a pair of fitted jeans and a tight black V-neck T-shirt. It was a good time of the month for my boobs, and I was taking full advantage. A little make-up, fix the hair… I was ready by the time Lynn rang the buzzer downstairs.

I slid into her two-door sports car and looked over with a smile. Tall, brown eyes, blond hair, a permanent twinkle in her eye, Lynn was a force of nature. There was no one better to go out drinking with. And she was a master wing woman.

"Ready?" she asked.

"Ready."

CHAPTER EIGHT

We settled on a place just outside the Plateau because it was a small, yet never too-crowded club. Drinks were priced mid-range, so you knew you were getting a decent class of guys. No cheapskates. Assholes and blowhards, maybe, but no cheapskates.

We walked into the club, and I was immediately swallowed up by the bass-heavy music. The weed was a creeper, and I was settling into a nice buzz as we approached the bar. There were cozy booths lining the wall, but they were dark and ill-placed for people-watching. We found two stools and climbed up. I ordered two gin and tonics, with a couple of shots of tequila to start.

"Huh," Lynn said. "I thought this was my idea. What's up?"

"If I'm going to do this, I'm going to do it properly," I said. "And I don't want to remember it tomorrow."

We downed the shots and started on our drinks. Lynn mumbled something about having to leave the car when I saw a blond-haired, blue-eyed guy on the dance floor, clearly checking me out. He was not my type, but he wasn't bad. I put my hand on Lynn's shoulder to shush her, and almost imperceptibly pushed my chin out in his direction. After waiting an appropriate amount of time, she turned to check him out.

"Go for it. I'll wait," she said. "Hey – can we get two more shots over here, please?" I smiled at her foresight and downed my shot. I finished my drink, watching him dance. A slow smile spread across his face as he caught me watching him. I put down my glass, got up, and headed over.

"Hi," he said.

"Hi."

He held out his hand, which I took, and he pulled me in close. He smelled rather good. He circled his arm around my waist, resting his hand on my hip as he swayed gently back and forth, brushing lightly against me. I closed my eyes, feeling his hand move across the small of my back.

I let the music carry me as we danced, and with my eyes closed, I imagined it was Matt holding me in his arms. I pressed myself closer against him, pushing my breasts up against his chest. He responded by cupping my ass. *I don't even know this guy's name.* I rested my hands on his shoulders, letting him guide me across the floor.

"Mind if I cut in?"

I opened my eyes, startled at the interruption. The alcohol, mixed with the pot, had taken effect and I was feeling no pain. I pulled back slightly, to see Pete standing there, smiling sheepishly. Blond hair/blue eyes looked nonplussed.

"Dude," he said. "We're dancing here."

I just laughed. I have no idea why. I started laughing and couldn't stop. Blond hair/blue eyes eyed me with a look that said, *Is crazy worth it?*

"Allie," Pete said. "You okay?"

"You know her, dude?"

"Yes, I know her," Pete said.

"All yours." And with that, my stallion was off. I was furious. But try as I might to hold on to that anger, I just kept dissolving into giggles. I was still swaying, so Pete took hold of my arms and danced with me.

"Who was that? What are you doing?" Pete asked.

"I'm out. Having fun. And this is no concern of yours," I added. "For Christ's sake. We went on four dates."

"Five. Allie, I could tell how drunk you are from across the room. You're going to get yourself in trouble," he said, concerned. Or jealous. In my state, it was hard to tell.

"Pete, Pete, Pete. You're wasting your time, Pete. Pete." I laughed.

"There you are!" Lynn said, coming up behind me and taking my arm. "Pete. Fancy meeting you here. Allie, come, let's go."

I smiled at Pete over my shoulder and let Lynn lead me back to the bar.

"Bye, Pete," I called, giggling.

There was a shot of tequila waiting for me. I smiled at Lynn.

"Thought you might need it," she said. "Where the hell did he come from?"

I downed the shot.

"No idea," I said. "He's probably out drinking with his friends."

Shit. His friends. Was Matt here? I put down my shot glass and signaled for another two. Lynn looked at me but downed her shot. I slammed my glass on the bar.

"I've got to go to the bathroom. I'll be right back."

"Want me to come with you?" Lynn asked.

"No. It's fine."

"If you're not back in seven minutes, I'm coming in after you," she said, setting an alarm on her phone.

I laughed and made my way down the bar. *What if he's here? What if he saw me? If he's here, and Pete saw me, of course he saw me. What if he's with a girl? What if he didn't see me because he's here with a girl? Or maybe he picked up a girl? Why not? I picked up a guy...*

I stood in front of the bathroom mirror, digging through my purse for my lipstick. If he was here, damn straight I was going to look my best. I tamed my hair, adjusted my cleavage, and headed back out.

CHAPTER NINE

Sure enough, Matt was there leaning up against the wall opposite the bathroom door. He was wearing a pair of faded jeans and a blue button-down, untucked. I imagined sliding my hands underneath it and running them up his chest. He smiled at me, like he knew exactly what I was thinking.

"I saw you on the dance floor," he said.

I blushed and looked down. I didn't know what to say. I hadn't done anything wrong, but I felt instantly ashamed. I felt the heat spread through my body and realized there was more than shame going on here.

"What are you doing here?" he asked.

I looked up at him, focusing on that small

scar. I clenched my fists to keep from reaching up to touch it. Just to run my finger along it. Just once. I took a step forward and stopped. What was I thinking?

"Trying to get you off my mind," I said.

It was not what I had intended to say, but apparently the tequila had vastly different ideas about how this scenario was going to play out.

"What are you doing here?" I countered.

"Trying to get you off Pete's mind," he said.

I took another step forward, as someone passed behind me on their way to the washroom. I stumbled slightly and regained my balance.

"You're drunk," he observed.

"Aren't you?"

"Designated driver. Stone-cold sober."

I nodded. At least one of us was capable of reason. I took another step, closing the gap. He straightened up against the wall.

"It killed me to watch you with that guy. Watching you press up against him like that," Matt said, looking me straight in the eye.

"Who? Blond hair/blue eyes?"

He laughed.

"Yes."

I put my hands on his shoulders and pressed myself up against him, as I had done on the dance floor.

"Like this?" I murmured in his ear.

He groaned. He drew a deep breath and using both hands, pushed me gently away.

"Yes. Just like that," he said. "Christ."

He reached up and rubbed the scar. I positively ached to touch it myself. Four, five shots of tequila, a gin and tonic, some killer weed... *fuck it.* He dropped his hand and I tentatively reached up and ran my index finger across it, feeling the slight ridge, and then feeling it disappear as his skin became smooth again. He grabbed my wrist.

"What are you doing?" he asked, his voice husky.

"I've been wanting to do that since I first met you."

"You're drunk."

"What's the matter? You're the one who came on to me. Twice. Now you're scared?"

"Now you're drunk. And Pete decided not to opt for outrage." Matt said.

"Ah. Heartbreak it was then."

I peered out towards the bar, trying to see if I could spot him. I turned back towards Matt.

"Dave's got him busy at the table," Matt said, reading my mind.

"So. You got Dave to occupy Pete, you waited outside the bathroom for me, and now you're saying you intended for nothing to happen?"

Matt was silent for a moment.

"I just wanted to see you," he whispered.

I closed my eyes for a moment and swayed slightly as I did so. I opened my eyes and smiled.

"Whoa…" I said, still swaying.

I put my hand out towards the wall by his head to steady myself. My face was inches away from his. I looked into those green eyes. There was nothing there but lust. I swallowed. I knew in the moment, despite being incredibly drunk, that he was using all his willpower not to kiss me. I was determined not to look away first. I parted my lips slightly as my heart beat faster and I felt the soft rise and fall of my chest.

Suddenly, he reached out and pulled me towards him. He cupped the back of my head, drew me in closer, and kissed me. He was gentle at first, then more insistent. He put both hands behind my head, fingers losing themselves in my hair. His tongue reached out, questioning, and I opened my mouth in answer, inviting him in. I pressed up against him once more, and this time his body welcomed me. When we came up for air I just grinned like an idiot.

"Thank god you know how to kiss," I said.

He looked at me, brushing a stray curl away from my face, and burst out laughing. He leaned in again, kissing me thoroughly, as if to confirm I'd drawn the right conclusion. He pushed me away.

"And that's enough of that," he said.

"What?" I said, incredulous. "What are you talking about. It's dark, we're alone, I'm drunk, we will never have this chance again."

"Yeah, it's that last thing that bothers me."

"Never having this chance again?"

"Well, that too. But I was referring to the drunk part."

"Oh. I'm okay. Don't worry about me. You have my full consent here. You think I've never fooled around with anyone while drunk? Why do you think I came here tonight?"

"I don't want to be blond hair/blue eyes."

"Holy shit. That's what I've been calling him in my head. How did you know that?"

"Because you just said it. Two minutes ago. You really are drunk."

I moved in and putting both hands on his shoulders pushed him up against the wall. I reached up and kissed him, refusing to allow him to move until I felt him melt into the kiss. His arms went around me, hands exploring, moving up and down along my back and sides.

He paused when he reached my breast, and cupping it in his hand, passed his thumb over my nipple. My stomach did a summersault and I felt a familiar ache between my legs. I pressed in closer against him.

"Well, hello. What's going on here?"

Jesus. Second time I'm busted in one night. I turn around to see Lynn standing there with the most bizarre look on her face. She looked Matt over, taking time in her evaluation.

"What the fuck, Allie?" she said. "Seven minutes. I said seven minutes."

I pulled away from Matt but stood partially in front of him, protecting him from the wrath of Lynn.

"Lynn. Meet Matt. Matt, Lynn."

I really didn't know what else to say. I'm not sure why I never mentioned him to Lynn before this. She'd been my best friend for fifteen years and knew everything about me. I thought maybe it had to do with knowing I could never see him again. Talking about him made him real.

"You know each other?" she asked.

"Yes," I said.

"From *before* tonight?" she asked again.

"Yes," I said again. "Do me a favour. Go back to the bar. Give me five minutes. Make sure Pete doesn't head this way."

Lynn looked at me, hesitant. Matt smiled at her.

"She's drunk," Lynn said.

"I know," he said. "I am 100 percent sober. We are fine."

"He won't touch me," I said.

Lynn burst out laughing.

"Seems like he was doing a pretty good job of it to me," she said.

"I will not take advantage of this woman," Matt said. "I promise you. You're a good friend. You can watch us from the bar. If she's not back in five minutes, come get her."

Lynn nodded, looking Matt over again with a new eye. She turned and walked away, looking back only once to make sure I was okay. I smiled and waved.

"So," Matt said.

"So."

The spell was broken, but the electricity between us was still there. I reached out again to trace the scar, thrilled that I was actually able to do so. My nipples hardened against the thin cotton of my T-shirt.

"Stop that," he said, gently taking my hand away.

"It can't possibly turn you on as much as it does me," I said.

"Stop that!" he insisted. "You think this is

easy for me? You think I don't want to drag you out the back door and take you home right now? Believe me, I would show you a night you would never forget. I can do things to your body that will make you scream. But the problem is, *Pete* lives at my home. And no, don't say we'll go to your place. That's not the point, and you know it. Besides, you're drunk."

I was drunk. So drunk I didn't care about Pete anymore. My entire being pulsed with how badly I wanted Matt. I could still feel his hands on my body. But I knew he was right.

"So that's it then," I said.

"That's it."

"Kiss me again."

"Are you always this forward?" he asked, amused.

"You'll have to find out. Kiss me. One more time. Come on, in for a penny…"

I smiled up at him. He sighed, but he leaned down and kissed me. He pulled away before I could get my arms around his neck.

"I made a promise to your friend. You wouldn't want me to break that promise, would you?" he asked. I shook my head. "Which one of us is leaving? We can't both stay."

"I'll go," I said.

"You're sure you're done picking up blond

haired, blue-eyed boys?" he asked, eyes twinkling.

"Yes. What about you? Going to stick around and see what you can find?"

I was half-joking, and I only said it because I was drunk, but my entire being was on edge awaiting his answer.

"No," he said, looking me in the eye. "We'll stick around, yes. But I'm good."

He looked over my shoulder and gave a slight nod. I turned to look, and Lynn was standing there, tapping the imaginary watch on her wrist with a stern expression on her face. Matt laughed and gave me a pat on the ass.

"You better go," he said. "She looks like someone you don't want to mess with."

CHAPTER TEN

I spent the cab ride home telling Lynn all the sordid details of how I met Matt, and the ridiculous situation we'd found ourselves in.

"It's not fair, Lynn. Matt's the rebound I should've had. Not Pete."

"Well, given the circumstances, I'd say that ship has sailed. You ended up with Rebound Pete. Deal with it."

"What? You didn't like Matt?"

"Oh, I liked him. But he's living with your ex-boyfriend. It's not worth the aggravation."

"Pete wasn't my boyfriend. And Matt's the first guy I've been attracted to since Josh."

"Well, that can't be true. You must have been attracted to Pete at some point."

"Pete was an act of desperation."

We both sat silently as the car weaved through the city streets.

"You still miss Josh?" Lynn asked, quietly.

"Sometimes."

The alcohol was wearing off and I was faced with the grim realization that despite all the opportunity I'd encountered that evening, I was *still* going home alone.

"It's normal, you know. You two were together for a long time. You were in love. It's not like either of you fell out of love..."

"No. He just didn't love me enough to commit."

Lynn said nothing. There was nothing to say. The cab pulled up outside my apartment building.

"You okay to manage on your own?" she asked.

"Yeah, I'm fine. Trish walked Loki earlier. I'm going straight to bed."

Trish was the 24-year-old temporarily living next door with her parents. She'd just gotten out of a bad relationship and needed love, support, and a warm bed. She and Loki had really taken to each other, and she walked her often. I got out of the car and paused, turning around.

"Thanks for coming tonight. I'm sorry I

didn't tell you about Matt."

"It's all good, my friend. I knew you'd get there eventually."

Lynn closed the car door as the cab pulled away.

I let myself into the apartment, Loki waiting patiently by the door for me.

"Do you sit here all night?" I asked her.

She let out a soft bark in reply. I laughed and walked to the bathroom, pulling off clothing as I went. I picked up the roach I'd left in the ashtray as I was getting ready and finished it off as I removed my makeup and put up my hair. I brushed my teeth and got into bed, turning on the TV for distraction. I was in no state to go over the evening's events just yet.

After a couple of episodes of *C.S.I.*, I shut off the tube and rolled over, trying to get some sleep. Loki lay at the foot of the bed, snoring quietly. I heard the buzz of my phone on the nightstand just as I was drifting off. I considered ignoring it, but curiosity got the better of me. I picked up the phone and checked my texts.

Allie?

I didn't recognize the number. And then it hit me. I didn't recognize the number.

Yes... who's this?

It's Matt.

My pulse quickened and I sat up in bed.

How did you get my number?

I pulled it off Pete's phone. He's dead drunk.

Ah.

You sobered up yet?

I laughed. He was certainly principled.

Pretty much. I'll be in trouble in the morning, though.

No doubt.

There was nothing for several minutes and I almost put the phone back down on the nightstand. The thought of him texting hadn't occurred to me. I didn't know if I was thrilled or upset. This would certainly make things harder. On the other hand…

Listen. I'm sorry about tonight. I shouldn't have kissed you.

I stared at the phone for a moment, considering.

I liked it.

I did, too. But it shouldn't have happened. And it can't happen again. Pete was really distraught after seeing you tonight. I can't do this to him.

My heart stopped.

I understand.

I waited a few minutes, put down the phone and went to sleep.

I spent the next day trying to work, but my eyes kept drifting to my phone. I had his number. I could reach him anytime I wanted. The thought was intoxicating. But what good would come of it? He'd made it clear – this was a non-starter.

I turned back to my computer, determined to get the review done. I tried to summon up memories of delicious dumpling soup and an exquisite sesame chicken, but all I could conjure were images of Matt, leaning up against the wall in the club, waiting for me. Giving up, I grabbed the leash and took Loki for a walk.

I ended up getting the work done, but what should've taken me two hours ended up taking seven. Not a good work-to-dollar ratio. Another way this guy was bad for me. I made myself a quick dinner of scrambled eggs and toast and snuggled into bed with Loki. I flipped on the TV and found a steamy episode of my favourite period drama. If I wasn't getting any Matt Goldberg, I could at least get some kilted Scotsman.

CHAPTER ELEVEN

Weeks went by and the days got even hotter as July turned into August. The sun was shining almost every day, but thankfully humidity was low. Work kept me busy as restaurants changed their menus for the latter half of the season, and I started toying with the idea of a writing a column on the side. Restaurant critic was fine, but it wasn't the end goal. There was more creative work to be done, and I thought a column would be the perfect forum for me.

I was enjoying a second glass of wine on a rooftop restaurant with Lynn as we polished off the last of the dessert.

"Lord, that was good," Lynn said. "Five stars."

"You're a great critic, there," I laughed, and then grew serious. "Listen, I'm thinking of pitching a column to Sarah."

Lynn eyed me.

"About what?" she asked.

"Well, that's the thing. I want a forum to write. I'm more than just restaurant reviews. I just haven't found my angle yet, and I can't pitch her until I know I've got something good."

"Well, I think that's great. You're a talented writer, Allie. I'm sure you'll come up with something."

I motioned to the waiter. He came over and started clearing the table.

"Could I get a glass of water, please?"

He nodded and headed off to the kitchen.

"See?" I said. "Right there. I called him over to ask him for something, and he started clearing the table. I didn't ask him to clear the table. I gave no indication we were done. Dammit. Why can't the food and the service align more often?"

"Seriously? You're going to hold that against them in the review? Allie, you need to get laid."

I blushed. Why did I always blush? No one in my family does that. It's the worst tell on the planet. So unfair.

"Allie... What are you not telling me?" Lynn asked.

"Nothing."

"Are you seeing Matt?"

"No. He won't have anything to do with me. Bro code."

"Good. At least one of you has sense."

The waiter returned with our water. I shook my head as he left without asking if we wanted anything else.

"Listen," I said. "You made it abundantly clear the other night what you thought about this whole situation. Can we just put it away for now and enjoy each other's company?"

"Well. When you put it like that," Lynn said, laughing. She checked her phone. "Shit, I have to get back to work. When's our next date?"

I dug into my bag and pulled out my notebook. Lynn rolled her eyes.

"You have a phone, you know."

I ignored her and looked down my list of restaurants, trying to pick one for our next lunch. My eye stopped on one – *Le petit train*, a French bistro that opened at the old abandoned train station outside Hudson. It was the oddest place to open a restaurant, though the parking would be easy out of the city. I was curious to check it out.

"How about *Le* –" I started and stopped

suddenly.

"Le what?" she said.

"Never mind. I'm not in the mood for French these days. How about the new Italian place on St. Laurent? Next Tuesday?"

"Sounds great," Lynn said. She reached for her bag and stood up. "I'll speak to you later."

She blew me a kiss and took off. I looked back down at my notebook and picked up my phone.

Matt? I've got an idea.

I waited a few minutes.

I'm at work.

Can you get off Friday afternoon for a few hours?

Allie, we can't see each other.

Trust me. This will be fine.

Allie.

You know that old train station in Hudson?

Yeah.

They just turned it into a restaurant. Opened last week. No one even knows about it yet. Meet me there, Friday at 1 pm.

Allie.

Come on. It's a public place, and it's far away. We're safe from Pete, we're safe from each other.

The waiter brought the bill over and I paid it, all while waiting for Matt's answer. I was putting my notebook back in my bag and getting ready to go when my phone finally buzzed.

Let me think about it.

A slow smile spread across my face. We were going to lunch.

*

By late that night, I hadn't heard back from Matt. Sleep was impossible. Maybe the whole idea had been a mistake. The two of us, in close proximity, with that heat between us. He had been smart not to get back to me. I shouldn't have texted him. He made it clear, I should've respected his wishes. If the situation were reversed, I'd have been screaming stalker.

So there was to be no lunch with Matt. What did I think would happen, anyway? That he'd jump me in the middle of the restaurant? That we'd make out in the parking lot? God, that kiss…

Without even thinking about it, my finger started making small circles on my belly, moving slowly upwards. I closed my eyes and cupped my breast, sliding further down under the sheets. The way his lips felt on mine, so soft and full. And he tasted of mouthwash and beer and pure passion. I ran my thumb over my nipple, feeling it harden under my touch. I imagined it was Matt's touch, his fingers tracing a line over my chest, past my navel, down...

I arched my back, raising my hips off the bed. I felt the cool, crisp cotton sheet rub against my breasts. A slight breeze came in from the window, carrying the scent of the lilac tree outside. I pictured us back in that dark club, his hands sliding over my body while whispering how much he wanted me. I pressed myself into my hand, sliding my middle finger inside while rubbing my palm against my clitoris.

My phone buzzed. Matt! I shot up, smiled to myself, and picked up the phone to check my texts.

Hey.

Hey, yourself.

What are you doing?

What was I doing? Talk about a moment of truth. He was texting to tell me he wasn't going to meet me. He'd probably been hoping I was already asleep and would only see it in the morning. Well, the coward wasn't going to get the easy way out. He wanted to know what I was doing?

I was just about to come.

Silence.

Are you alone?

Yes.

I'm sorry I interrupted you.

I'm not.

Allie…

Just shut up, Matt. I'm here. Naked. Tell me what you want me to do.

Another silence. Had I taken it too far?

Describe to me where you are.

Bingo!

I'm in my bed. The room is dark, and there's a breeze coming in from the open window.

Were you thinking about me, before I called?

Yes.

What were you thinking?

I was thinking about you kissing me. How your hands felt on my body. How badly I wanted you.

What were you doing?

I was touching myself, Matt. I was so close to coming.

And you want me to bring you there again?

Yes.

You looked so hot that night, Allie.

Tell me.

You were wearing that tight black T-shirt, showing off all your curves. I could barely keep my hands off you.

I wish you hadn't…

Watching you on the dance floor, seeing you move, seeing you press yourself up against that guy…

Did it turn you on?

God, I wanted you.

I was pretending he was you. That it was your body I was rubbing myself against.

When I saw you, outside the bathroom, I wanted to slam you up against the wall.

Here we go.

I wanted you to, Matt.

I wanted to run my hands all over your body, every inch. Wrap them up in your hair and kiss you. I could practically taste you.

Matt…

I remember how hard your nipple got as soon as I touched you. I want you to rub your nipple now, like I did. Can you do that?

Yes.

I can just picture you, on your bed, naked.

Well. He certainly rose to the occasion. I did as commanded.

Matt, this is so hot.

Trace a line down your stomach, slowly. I want you to touch yourself. Reach between your legs and tell me if you're wet.

I am so wet, Matt. God, I wish you were here.

What would you do if I were?

I'd take you in my mouth. I have been dying to wrap my mouth around you. God, I would make you come so hard.

Come for me now, Allie.

Oh, god, Matt.

At least five minutes went by with complete radio silence. I stared at the ceiling, in complete shock at what just happened. At what I just did. I started it. And for all I know he's some crazed sociopath. I don't even know what he does for a living.

Matt, what do you do for a living?

What?

Answer me.

I'm a network architect.

Okay. Crazy people aren't network architects, right?

Allie? Are you okay?

I think so. I came pretty hard there.

Lol.

Why'd you text me?

Silence.

To say yes to lunch.

CHAPTER TWELVE

I was wearing a black spaghetti strap sundress with small white flowers printed on it. It was fitted on top, then flared out, falling at the knee. I'd bought it for the twirl, even though at 31, I never twirled. But there was something whimsical about it and I only wore it when I was feeling a little mischievous. What I was about to do was certainly wrong.

I drove to the restaurant, purposefully early so that I could scope the place out and get my initial notes down before I had to go in. I never take notes during a meal. The restaurant, if possible, should never suspect a critic in the house.

There were quite a few cars in the parking

lot, which surprised me. I pulled into a spot and pulled out my notebook, just to write down early impressions and expectations, which I loved to later compare with my finished review. I looked up from writing just in time to see Matt about to enter the restaurant. My heart almost stopped. I had forgotten how beautiful he was. He was in jeans and a black T-shirt and was talking to someone on his cell phone. The curve of his shoulder and the flex of muscle in his upper arm as he pulled the door open was enough to turn my insides to jelly. I waited a few moments, checked my reflection in the mirror and got out of the car.

He was sitting in a booth at the back of the restaurant, facing the door. He was absorbed in the menu and didn't notice me come in. There were two glasses of white wine on the table. He reached for his and not finding the stem, broke his gaze from the menu to look. Having done so, he caught my eye and smiled. I made my way over to the table and sat down across from him.

"You look beautiful," he said.

"So do you," I said.

He laughed.

"I didn't know if you liked red or white. I figured I'd order white, and we could switch to red with the food if you'd prefer. I didn't want to be presumptuous, I'm sorry. I just figured tequila shots weren't appropriate and I'm nervous as fuck," he said. I was charmed.

Things were awkward between us, so the wine was handy. Not only was it the first time we'd been alone, face to face, but our steamy sexting session hung between us like a thick fog. I squirmed in my seat just thinking about it and decided to open conversation in a neutral direction.

"White is fine," I said. "Let me explain how this works."

"Works?" he asked, clearly confused.

"Yes. The ordering," I said.

"You're going to tell me how to order my food?" He looked at me like I was nuts. "I know how to eat in a restaurant."

I laughed.

"With a food critic?" I asked.

"Ah."

"Right. So, order whatever you want, but it can't be what I'm having. You need to order at least two appetizers and two mains. I'll do the same. You can try mine and I can try yours. Save room for dessert. I prefer to have the waiter or sommelier recommend the wine, but if you have favourites, that's fine."

"Wow. You're not a cheap date," he laughed.

"I'm paying," I said.

"Ah!" he said. "I like this."

"Yeah, just don't let Lynn find out. She'd kill you. She loves French food."

I looked over the menu and gave the waiter my order, then watched as Matt did the same. That scar. As if reading my mind again, he reached up to rub it. He then asked the waiter to recommend a wine, and I smiled. *He learns quick.*

The waiter gone, we found ourselves alone once more. There were about twenty tables in the restaurant, eleven of them currently full. I couldn't believe how quickly word had gotten out. It was a soft launch, yet... I hoped the food would be good. I looked over at Matt and smiled.

"This is nice," I said.

He smiled.

"Tell me about your work," he said.

I shrugged.

"What's there to tell? I eat, I write about it. I try not to put on too much weight. I've been at it for five years now."

"Do you like it? I mean, it seems like a dream job to me..."

"I do, but I want more. This was supposed to be a stepping-stone, a foot in the door... I don't want to write about other peoples' food forever. I want to write about me, my own experiences."

"So why don't you?" he asked, clearly interested.

I smiled.

"I'm thinking about it. I just have to figure some things out," I said. "What about you? Do you like what you do?"

"I do. I love working with technology. There are a lot of opportunities," he said.

"Like?"

He didn't say anything, and the waiter returned with our appetizers.

"Oh dear Lord," he said.

I smiled and reached over with my fork to stab a stray spear of asparagus on his plate. Popping it in my mouth I rolled my eyes back. "Delicious," I said.

We worked our way through the appetizers and gradually became more comfortable with each other. We were mid-way through the main courses when he reached over to fill my wine glass. I put out my hand and rested it on his bare forearm. He looked at me, then at his arm.

"I'm good on the wine," I said, not removing my hand.

He just looked at it, like it was burning a hole through his skin, bottle still suspended mid-air.

"Why did you agree to have lunch with me?" I asked.

He put down the bottle.

"I honestly don't know. I realize now it was a mistake. Especially after... All I want to do is kiss you. But I can't. And I won't. But at the same time, I'm really enjoying myself with you. This is a fucking tragedy."

"Of Shakespearean proportions," I agreed.

He laughed. I got up from my side of the table and slid onto the bench beside him. He stopped laughing and his face grew serious.

"What are you doing, Allie?"

"Don't worry. We're in a public place. Nothing is going to happen. We're safe here, remember?"

He looked over at me with suspicion in his eye. I put my hand on the table and he took it in both of his. He looked down and studied it, carefully massaging each of my fingers and circling his thumb on my palm. I leaned over and brushed my lips across his ear.

"I can't stop thinking about you," I whispered.

He swallowed and held my hand tightly between his own.

"Allie," he said.

I pulled away and leaned against the back of the bench.

"I know about the bro code. I get it."

"There's a reason I took the pantry."

"What?"

"The pantry. There's a reason I volunteered to take the pantry."

"Proximity to the fridge?" I asked.

He gave a gentle snort.

"Well, yeah, that too. But that wasn't the main reason."

I looked at him, questioningly.

"It's because we signed a year lease, and I'm going to be gone for six months this year. I leave in September. I guess I figured this would be my last chance to see you before I left."

So there it was. I looked down, taking in this information. I pushed my plate away, no longer hungry. A million conflicting thoughts ran through my head. *Oh no!* was quickly followed by *Problem solved!*

But the more I tried to focus on the latter, the more my thoughts drifted to the former.

"Where are you going?" I asked.

"The Netherlands. Amsterdam, actually. We've got a client I'm consulting for."

"You'll be in Amsterdam for six months?"

"Well, not exactly. I'll be doing some traveling around Europe."

"Wait.   This   isn't   some

Chandler/Janice/Yemen thing, is it?"

Matt turned in his seat to look at me.

"No. This is not some Yemen thing. I am going to the Netherlands for six months to do some consulting. I will be gone come September. End of story."

"Let's skip dessert," I said. I called the waiter over and asked for the bill. I couldn't bear the thought of sitting there for a minute longer. We got up from the table and Matt moved towards the front entrance. I put out my hand and pulled him back by the belt buckle loop on his jeans. He turned to me, questioning.

"Let's go out the back. I need to see the gardens," I said.

CHAPTER THIRTEEN

The front exterior of the restaurant was all parking lot, but once through the back door, we found ourselves in a beautiful garden on the edge of the woods. The tracks still ran along the far edge of the garden, even the though the train ran no more. For décor, or nostalgia reasons, the owners decided to leave the wooden shelter on the old train platform in place, and a bench remained underneath it.

I took Matt's hand and led him towards the shelter. As we walked through the garden I mentally went through my options. We said goodbye now, and I spared myself the risk of pain, or I seized this moment and made the most of it. I could practically hear Lynn whispering in my ear about being a grownup. I needed to make responsible decisions. I frantically searched my mind for some compromise.

I sat down, and he sat beside me. Our backs were towards the restaurant, which lay beyond the garden. We were secluded. It was mid-afternoon and the sun was hot and high in the sky. The shelter provided some relief, but a light sweat broke out on my skin. I ran my tongue over my lower lip, tasting the last remaining traces of the pinot grigio we'd had with lunch.

"What are you thinking?" Matt asked.

"Nothing," I said. "Everything. Let's just sit here quietly for a moment."

We sat and listened to the birds in the forest as they went about their business. The more time passed, the more I became aware of his body next to mine. We were barely touching, and the small amount of space between us was charged with electricity. I thought about his mouth on mine and my nipples hardened instantly. I licked my lips and tried to steady myself. *Fuck it.*

I put my right hand on his leg. I left it there for a moment, feeling the heat transfer between our bodies. He picked it up gently and put it back down on my own knee. So that was off the table.

I thought about our text conversation and let the warmth flow from my hand into my leg. Slowly, I ran my thumb up and down along the inside of my thigh. I felt Matt tense beside me, but he said nothing.

Slowly, I drew my hand up along my thigh, pushing aside my dress.

"What are you doing?" he whispered, his voice strained.

"Nothing we didn't do by text," I whispered back, looking him straight in the eye. My hand disappeared under my dress and I closed my eyes.

"Allie," he said. I opened my eyes and gave him my most innocent look.

"I seem to have forgotten my underwear," I said quietly.

"Oh, god," he said.

I turned to face him. I rested one arm along the back of the bench and pulled my knee up. His eyes traveled down my body, following my hand as I rubbed myself lightly, flat-palmed.

I tilted my head and looked at him, feeling incredibly erotic outside in the open air, touching myself while he watched. I slid two fingers inside and moaned softly, closing my eyes for a moment as I rolled my hips up and started to move.

I opened my eyes to find him staring at me, desire emanating from his body. He reached out and lightly brushed his finger across my breast. I arched my back slightly, feeling his touch spread throughout my body.

"Nothing we haven't done before," he whispered.

"Oh, god, Matt..."

"Let me see you, Allie."

I pushed my dress higher up, opening my legs wider to give him a better view. I slowly slid my fingers in and out, using my thumb to rub up against my sweet spot. I could feel my pulse quicken, and the tension build.

"Does this turn you on, Allie? Me, watching you?"

"Yes."

"Good. I want to watch you come."

"Come with me," I said, slowing down.

He fumbled with his zipper. I breathed heavily as he reached in and took himself in hand. God, every part of him was beautiful. He stroked himself, slowly at first, and as he built up speed, I increased my own. I wanted to wait, but I was so far ahead of him.

"Matt–" I cried. He moved in, covering my mouth with his. He freed his hand to pull me closer, holding me firmly against him as my body convulsed. When it was over, I rolled my eyes up towards the sky and let out a short laugh.

"Holy shit," I said.

I looked over at him and smiled, and saw the lust still shining in his eyes. I looked down and realized he hadn't finished. He removed his arm from around my shoulders and took himself firmly in hand. He locked eyes with me and started stroking himself once more. I brought my hand up slowly and used my pinky to slide the spaghetti strap off my shoulder. His gaze turned downward, to watch what I was doing. He was breathing very heavily, using his other hand to support himself against the back of the bench.

I slowly traced my finger along the top of my dress. With just the slightest pressure, I pushed down the fabric, revealing the top of my breast. He closed his eyes momentarily as he tried to slow his breathing. By the time he opened them, I had worked the top of the dress down and was holding my breast in my hand, rubbing my nipple between my thumb and index finger. The look in his eyes made me feel like a goddess, and I gave him my best seductive smile.

"Nothing we haven't done before," I said. "That's how you wanted it, right?"

He took his left hand off the back of the bench and reached out to touch me. I shivered and pushed myself into his hand. He moaned, taking hold of my breast and squeezing. Without even thinking about it, I reached between his legs and put my hand over his right hand, following his up and down motions with increasing speed.

"Oh god, Allie," he moaned. "Oh, god. Use your mouth."

He didn't have to ask twice. I immediately dropped to the ground before him. I gently unwrapped his fingers and took him in my mouth. He tasted sweet and salty and I felt a thrill in my stomach as I took him deeper. I looked up and noticed his eyes were closed.

"Matt," I said. "Watch me."

He opened his eyes and moaned as I took him in my hand and ran my tongue from the base up to the tip. If there was one thing I could do for him, it was this. His breathing came faster, and I felt his fingers wind their way through my hair. I took him into my mouth once again, focusing on the work at hand. One of his hands left my hair and reached down to find my breast. I moaned, and I felt him constrict at the same moment he cried out.

When he was done, I pulled my head away,

and gingerly wiped the corner of my mouth. I wrapped my arms around his calves and rested my cheek on his knee.

"That's something we haven't done before," he said. I let out a soft laugh. I let go of his legs and pulled my dress back up. I was about to get up on my feet when he reached out and took my elbow. "Hey, you're really good at that. *Really* good."

I smiled and stood, straightening myself up. After a moment, he got up and zipped up his jeans. He looked me in the eye, then leaned in and kissed me. I wrapped my arms around his neck and closed my eyes, letting myself get lost in the moment. Never would I meet another man who kissed like this.

He pulled away and laughed. "This was a terrible brilliant idea, Allie. Congratulations."

"You can't tell me you're sorry you came," I said, eyes gleaming. "Pun intended."

"No. Definitely not sorry," he said.

We were quiet for a moment.

"Maybe Pete will have met someone by the time I get back," he said suddenly.

I laughed.

"We're talking seven months in the future here. You think you won't have met someone by then? You'll be traveling, Matt. Free as a bird. Let's not pretend this is something it's not."

He dropped my hand and looked at me.

"Something it's not?"

He looked hurt, but I didn't back down.

"I thought Pete was the only problem here," he said. "I don't date a lot, Allie. My work kind of makes relationships difficult. I like you. I haven't been interested in anyone in years. What do you think this is exactly?"

"This is fun. You're about to leave. We don't even know each other."

And in that moment, I realized we didn't. Why was there drama suddenly? I avoided drama. Yet there I was, at the height of it – starting a semi-affair with the roommate of the guy I just broke up with. Who was also about to leave the continent for six months. I couldn't understand how I let this happen.

"Look," I said, suddenly impatient. "All I do know is I have to go home and write up a restaurant review. Without having tasted one fucking dessert."

Matt looked at me, clearly at a loss. I wasn't in the mood to help him out.

"Let's go," I said, and turned back towards the restaurant.

CHAPTER FOURTEEN

When I got home, I was surprised not to find Loki at the front door waiting for me. I put down my keys and my purse, calling her name – nothing. I was worried for a moment until I remembered I'd asked Trish to walk her. I'd had higher hopes for the afternoon than what had actually played out. *Fuck.*

I walked to the living room and opened the window to try to get some air into the stifling apartment. What the hell had just happened? Everything was amazing. Did he fuck that up? Did I? Six months? Six months! I was working myself into a good rage when I heard the knock on the door. I went to open it, finding Trish and Loki on the other side. Trish handed me the leash and then put a small box she was holding down on the entryway table.

"Thanks, Trish. I really appreciate it. I didn't think I'd be home so soon," I said.

"No problem," she said. "Anytime. You know how much I love that dog."

She turned to go.

"What's in the box?" I asked.

Already out of the apartment, she turned to face me.

"Oh," she said. "I bumped into some guy outside, he asked if you lived here. I told him yes, and he asked me to give it to you."

I thanked her and picked up the box. Carrying it in the kitchen, I tried to figure out what was in it by gauging its weight. Not heavy, but not light, either. I put it on the kitchen table and opened it, finding nestled inside two desserts – a slice of chocolate cake, and a fruit tart. There was a note on the side.

Allie, I don't know what just happened, but I don't want to fuck up your review. Hope these will do.

I couldn't help it. I had to smile. I picked up my phone and texted him.

Thank you.

*

I buried myself in work over the next few weeks. Working up my courage, I finally went to see my editor, Sarah, about a new column. She didn't seem very receptive to the idea but agreed to hear me out when I had a refined pitch. I spent a lot of time trying to do exactly that, but it was difficult when my thoughts kept being interrupted by the memories of warm hands, sea-green eyes, and that tiny scar.

He didn't text, and I didn't expect him to. He'd finally laid out the cards. There was clearly no road forward. I picked up the phone and dialed.

"Lynn?" I said, when she finally picked up. "Let's go out tonight."

Ever the best friend, she was downstairs within thirty minutes. This time, I suggested a spot far from the beaten path. No way I wanted to risk running into Matt again.

We found a place about 15 minutes outside the downtown core. A neighbourhood favourite with good music and Tanqueray behind the bar. It was a Friday night and it was packed with people finishing off a long work week. We edged our way in and found two seats – a minor miracle in itself. Lynn ordered the drinks and I swiveled around in my stool, to check out the action on the dance floor.

It was a lively crowd, and the dancing was

raucous. Yet despite that, off to the side, were two women dancing together, very slowly and awfully close. One was a brunette with straight hair and the longest legs I'd ever seen. The other was a redhead, soft curls cascading down her shoulders. The had their arms around each other's waists and were staring into each other's eyes. They had zero concern that the song was a fast one. They were lost in their own world. As evidence, the brunette leaned down and kissed the redhead, moving her hands from her waist to her shoulders as the redhead pressed herself up against her partner, responding in kind.

"Probably be a lot easier," Lynn remarked, following my gaze.

"I don't know. I'm not opposed to it, just not sure what to do with all the bits," I said, thoughtfully.

"Please. You're a woman. You do what you'd want done to you. And she'd be a woman. She'd tell you what you're doing wrong," Lynn said, and we both laughed.

I turned back to my drink, stirring the swizzle stick and listening to the ice clink, barely audible over the music. I felt him sit down beside me before I saw him. Then I heard Lynn gasp. I turned my head, and there he was. Josh. My ex. I really had to stop going to bars.

"Tanqueray and tonic?" he asked.

He signaled to the waiter and ordered two gin and tonics. He turned back to me. He looked just the same. Short, close-cropped black hair, dark eyes, fair skin, just shy of six feet. We were the perfect dance partners. He was dressed impeccably.

"How are you doing, Allie?"

It took me a moment before I could speak. The bartender put the drinks down on the bar and I took a long swallow before looking at him again.

"I'm great, Josh. How are you?"

"I'm good. It's been a... a long time," he said.

"That it has."

"How are you, Lynn?" Josh asked.

Lynn looked at him, unsure of how to react.

"Desperately in need of a bathroom. I'll be back."

She made her escape. I wished I could have followed. Josh was still staring at me. I reluctantly turned back to him.

"Are you here alone?" he asked.

"No. I'm here with Lynn."

He looked at me.

"Allie. You know what I mean."

"No, I'm not seeing anyone. At the

moment."

We were both silent for a few moments, drinking, listening to the music, trying to figure what, if anything, there was to say. Josh put down his drink.

"Let's dance."

I smiled, despite myself. I put down my glass and let him lead me to the dance floor. He took me into the middle of the crowd, and throngs of hot, sweaty bodies danced around us, moving in time with the heavy bass beat. Josh took me around the waist and pulled me close, moving against me. He'd always been such a good dancer.

I closed my eyes and let myself get lost in the music. I felt his hands move over my back and did nothing. We moved together, so close I could smell his familiar cologne, the scent of which unlocked a million memories in my mind.

He moved his head towards my neck, nuzzling me softly and pushing my hair out of the way. It just felt so good to be touched again, by someone who knew how, by someone who knew me.

"ALLIE!"

My eyes popped open and I saw Lynn standing over Josh's shoulder, furious.

"Josh," she said. "What the fuck are you

doing?"

Josh pulled back and had the decency to look ashamed. He held onto my hands and looked at me.

"Allie, I'm sorry. I just... I don't know. Seeing you..."

I pulled my hands free, allowing Lynn to bring me back to reality, back to the fact that no matter how I felt about the man standing before me, he would never commit to me. He simply couldn't.

"I get it," I said.

Lynn gently took my hand and led me away from the dance floor. I looked back over my shoulder and saw Josh standing there, watching after us. We walked towards the exit.

"I'm sorry, Lynn. I don't know what came over me."

"Loneliness."

CHAPTER FIFTEEN

In the cab ride home, Lynn studied me thoughtfully.

"You going to be okay?" she asked.

"I hope so. I can't believe that just happened."

"You're not that girl anymore," Lynn said softly. "You've grown up. It's time for you to figure that out."

Lynn's words stayed with me. When I got home, I made myself a smoothie and rolled a joint. I planned to knock myself out and wake up in the morning. I crawled into bed and picked up my phone to scroll Instagram before going to sleep. I put the phone down and shut the light. My phone buzzed.

You're okay?

Count on Lynn.

I'm fine, Lynn. Thanks for checking in. Love you.

Love you, too, babe.

I held the phone in my hand and went to my contacts list. I scrolled down until I found Josh and after only a second's hesitation, hit delete. I then went to Matt's chat window. It was blank. We had agreed to delete all our texts, neither of us wanting to be the keeper of evidence. I was suddenly deeply sorry for that agreement. Reading over those would've been a great way to get my mind off Josh.

On Monday morning I had a staff meeting, the rare occasion that I had to be in the office. I usually did my work from home, showing up only for meetings. On this day, however, I was there the entire afternoon. When everything shut down for the day, some of my colleagues invited me to join them for a drink at a nearby bar. I decided to go.

It was August 20th, over two weeks since I'd last seen, spoken, or texted with Matt. I sat at a table at the downtown bar, sipping my gin and tonic while half-listening to my colleagues. The place was filled with people, all eager to stop for a drink before heading home to their partners and families, or happy for a place to go to avoid the loneliness of home for just a little while longer.

The music was so loud I would never have heard my phone, but I had it on silent and felt it vibrate in my back pocket. I pulled it out, checked my texts, and caught my breath.

Allie. Let's talk.

I couldn't believe Matt was contacting me. It went against everything I thought I'd learned about him thus far. Yet there he was, reaching out. I looked around and then back down at my phone.

I'm in a crowded bar. Not quite the right time.

Silence.

But I will talk to you. Later.

I didn't want to discourage him, but I did want to buy myself some time to think things through.

Go outside.

I had this wild notion that somehow, he was standing outside, waiting for me. I grabbed my purse, mumbled some excuse to my colleagues and walked out the door. I stood outside, looking around, trying to see if I could spot him. My phone buzzed in my hand.

Are you outside?

Yes.

Not a second later the phone rang.

"What is it?" I asked. "Is everything okay?"

"Allie. He met someone," Matt said.

I was quiet for a moment as I let that sink in.

"When?" I asked.

"It's been about 10 days. They've been together every night. She's here right now," he said.

I stood absolutely still and held the phone to my ear. My blood ran hot through my body, leaving me with a racing heart and a dry mouth. *He met someone.*

"You know where I live. I'll be there in 20 minutes," I hung up the phone and hailed a cab.

CHAPTER SIXTEEN

When the cab pulled up outside my building, I saw him sitting on the front steps, waiting for me. He got up as I exited the car and smiled shyly. It threw me, until I realized I was responding in kind. We were free to do as we please now, and suddenly we were both nervous about what that meant.

"What's her name?" I asked him as I turned the key in the door.

"Diana," he said. "Dave introduced them. Got tired of watching him mope around over you for weeks on end."

I shook my head as we walked up the two flights to my apartment. I wasn't ready to be in the elevator with him.

"What did he even see in me?" I asked.

"Oh, I can think of a few things," he chuckled. I looked back over my shoulder at him and rolled my eyes.

"You know what I mean. There was zero chemistry between us," I said.

"Pete wants to get married. Period." Matt explained. He stood by while I fit the key into the lock of my apartment door. I opened it, flipped open the light, and greeted Loki, who was whining at Matt with a concerned look in her eyes.

"You've got a dog," he said. "A big dog."

"I'm a single woman living alone in the city. It's almost a prerequisite," I said, grabbing the leash. "Come, let's go for a walk."

"He's friendly?" he asked.

"She's very friendly. So long as you mean me no harm."

We locked eyes for a moment and my breath caught. He looked me up and down in that way he had and my knees went weak. I broke the spell by looking for my keys while he turned to head back into the hall.

We walked around the block, making small talk and getting to know more about each other. We talked about what he did for a living, and he asked me tons of questions about my work. We discussed our favourite books, movies, and TV shows. We compared music preferences and best concerts. As we rounded the corner, he took my free hand in his and gave it a slight squeeze. I smiled to myself and returned the squeeze. We began to fill each other in on the past couple of weeks but skirted around the subject of his upcoming trip.

When we got back up to the apartment, I unleashed Loki and after a quick drink, she went straight for the bedroom. I led Matt to the living room and we sat on the couch. He looked around, taking in the eclectic décor, while we tried to ignore the uncomfortable silence.

"Do you party?" I asked.

"Yes," he said, looking relieved. "What a great idea."

I went into the kitchen to get the box, and when I returned found him thumbing through my bookshelf. I sat on the couch and rolled a joint, lighting it up once done.

"Come sit beside me," I said.

He walked over and sat down. While taking the joint from my hand, he lightly brushed against my fingers. It felt like an electric shock. Our eyes met and I smiled. We sat quietly for a few moments, passing the joint back and forth. Each time our fingers touched the sparks returned. My heart was racing. He shifted slightly, and his left rested against mine. More sparks.

I felt I should say something to break the tension but I had no idea what. I knew that if I moved, I'd jump him. I wanted nothing more than to be in his lap, wrapping my legs around his waist and burying my hands in his shirt. My heart beat faster as this scenario played out in my head and I took a long, thoughtful drag on the joint.

Suddenly, Matt reached out and carefully took the joint from my fingers. He put it down in the ashtray and turned his attention to me. Cupping my chin in his palms, he tilted my face up towards his and kissed me. It was a long, slow kiss that awakened every molecule of my being. I lost myself in that kiss.

At some point, he broke away and looked me in the eye. I reached up and stroked his face, smiling at him.

"That doesn't get old," I said.

He laughed. He had this great laugh that made my insides come alive. What wouldn't I do to hear that laugh? And then I stopped. I wouldn't be hearing that laugh. It was the end of August – he'd probably be leaving soon.

He leaned down and kissed me again, this time using his hand to explore my back and torso, pulling me closer towards him on the couch. My hands found their way to his waist, worked their way under his shirt and up his back. I kissed his neck, shyly tasting his skin, then ran my tongue up to his ear, feeling the roughness of his jawline. I gently took his earlobe between my teeth, nibbling to my heart's content. He tasted delicious. He pulled away suddenly and looked at me. He motioned towards the hallway, to my bedroom.

"You want to…"

"No."

"No?"

He looked at me, a mix of surprise and confusion clouding his face.

"Let's stay here," I said. "Let's just make out."

He laughed, unsure.

"Allie, I'm all for taking things slow, but I've watched you come. I think we're past making out."

"That's not the point. Let's do this right."

"Allie. I'm leaving Saturday. I'm not sure we have the time to do this right."

I moved away from him on the couch. Saturday! That was in four days. *I'd say the ship sailed on that one.* It was like Lynn was in the room with me. I could hear her say the words.

"That's four days from now," I said. "I thought your departure was weeks away."

"I know. They moved up the contract."

"When were you planning on telling me?" I asked.

"I don't know. I just wanted to enjoy the evening with you."

I stood up and started pacing. I shouldn't do this. I couldn't do this. A rebound fling was one thing. Setting myself up for heartbreak was another.

I stopped pacing and looked at him. He was sitting on the couch, hands clasped between his knees. He was waiting for me to come to some sort of decision.

"I'm thinking maybe you should go," I said quietly.

He stood up.

"Understood," he said.

He walked towards the door, and I followed him, a good pace behind. I was worried that if I were close enough to touch him, to smell him, I'd cave and beg him to stay. He stopped when he got to the door and turned to look at me.

"I'm sorry, Allie," he said. "The timing… if things were different."

I just nodded and smiled at him. I reached out, despite myself, and touched his face lightly. He took a step towards me, and before I knew it, we were pressed up against the wall, making out like teenagers. I wanted him. I wanted to lead him to my bedroom and take off my clothes and let him do all kinds of unmentionable things to me. His hands were everywhere, in my hair, my shoulders, my breasts. His mouth on mine, his tongue exploring, searching. I could taste him, taste how badly he wanted me, too.

"Are you sure you want me to leave?" he asked, pulling away.

And the spell was broken. *Six months. Six months. Six months.* The voice was screaming in my head. I couldn't shut it out. I pulled away from him, reluctantly, using every ounce of willpower I had.

"Yes."

He stroked my hair, gave me one last smile, and walked out the door.

CHAPTER SEVENTEEN

I woke up the next morning and lay in bed, staring at the ceiling. Wednesday. I just had to get through the week, and he'd be gone. The entire situation would be out of my hands. I could do this. I kept busy, working all through the morning and taking Loki out to the dog park in the afternoon.

I stopped at Starbucks on the way home, enjoying an iced chai on the terrace and people-watching with my dog. It was a beautiful late summer day, the sun shining, and the breeze cool on my skin. The chai was heavenly – the perfect blend of sweet and spice, served cold.

I stopped for take-out at my favourite Indian place in the neighbourhood and brought it home for dinner. By the time I was done and filed my review, it was nine o'clock and I was able to convince myself that it was bedtime.

One down. Three to go.

By the next night I was climbing the walls. My brain was telling me I was halfway there, but my heart, and other bits, were telling me I'd wasted two precious days. I was alone. I couldn't call Lynn. I knew exactly what she'd say – and it was exactly what I didn't want to hear.

I couldn't stop thinking about our make-out session on the couch, in the hallway... yet I couldn't relax enough to just rub one out and put myself out of my misery. I was a walking ball of sex, like a pile of dry tinder just waiting to catch fire. I picked up the phone and dialed.

"Matt?" I said.

"Yeah."

"Come."

He hung up. I jumped in the shower and tried to ignore the fact that I'd probably just done the stupidest thing I'd ever done in my entire life. In less than forty-eight hours, he'd be gone. But I shivered at the thought of what we could do in that time.

I was still in my robe, drying my hair when the buzzer rang. I walked down the hall and hit the button to let him in. My body was pulsing, and I tried to steady my breathing before he walked through the door. I swear I felt him approach before I heard the knock. I moved forward, as if in a dream, and turned the handle to let him in.

He walked in, took one look at me, and stopped in his tracks. I was still in my robe, which hung partially open, revealing one breast almost to the nipple. My hair, only towel-dried and still damp, hung around my shoulders, dripping water slowly down the front of my chest. He closed the door slowly behind him and turned to look at me, hunger in his eyes.

"Take that off," he said.

I pulled the belt and let the robe drop to the floor. I was completely naked underneath, but I felt zero shame. The way he was looking at me, that mixture of lust and reverence, made me feel sexy as fuck. I ran my tongue over my lower lip, watching him to see what he'd do next. He just stood there, staring at me, devouring me with his eyes. Anticipation bubbled up within me, spreading throughout my body until I felt as if I was supercharged, that one touch would send me over the edge. I pressed my hand flat against my belly, aching to touch myself, give myself some degree of relief.

He was on me in a minute, taking my hands and pinning me against the wall with his body. He leaned forward and kissed me, and tiny little explosions went off in my head. I kissed him back, hungrily, releasing my hands from his grip and wrapping my arms around his neck. I pressed myself up against him, trying to coax him into taking me right there, in the hallway.

"In the bedroom," he said. "Now."

He disentangled my arms from his neck and backed away. He made a grand gesture with his arm, indicating I should lead the way. I walked into my bedroom and turned to look at him.

"Lie down. On your stomach."

I didn't question him. There was something so hot about being naked while he was fully clothed. I settled onto the bed, folding my arms to make a pillow for my head. He stood there for a moment, just watching me, drinking me in. Then he walked over and sat down on the edge of the bed. He reached over and put one hand on my leg, right at the ankle. He let it sit there for a minute, then started running it up my calf, my knee, my thigh, stopping just underneath my ass. He repeated the action on my other leg. I could barely keep still.

"You don't have to keep still," he said,

reading my mind. "And you don't have to keep quiet."

I sighed. All he'd done was talk to me and run his hands up my legs and I was on the verge of orgasm. He cupped my ass, me squirming beneath his touch. He traced the curves of my back with his fingers.

"Your skin is so soft," he murmured. "I have wanted to touch you like this for so long."

I moaned in response. It seemed to be the only sound I was capable of. He continued to run his hands along my body, taking one arm, then the other, from underneath my head and caressing, rubbing, until all the blood in my veins was on fire.

"I want to feel every inch of you, every part of you. Turn over."

"Why are you doing this? Just fuck me," I pleaded.

"Well, I could ask you what you like, or I could let your body tell me. It's much more fun to let your body tell me."

"Can't you just fuck me? We can do all this later, I promise."

"Patience."

He waited while I turned over. Taking one of my hands in his, he traced the lines on my palm. I closed my eyes.

"Open your eyes."

I opened my eyes. He was working his hands up along my arm and then running his fingers lightly over my chest, making me arch my back and groan.

"Please…"

"Shhh," he said.

He ran one finger down between my breasts, down my stomach, and then wrapped the flat of his palm along the side of my waist. Turning his hand so his fingers pointed downward, he worked it down my leg, stopping to squeeze my thigh lightly, thumb edging its way between my legs. I tried to position myself so that he'd be forced to touch me. He just laughed and gave me a light swat between the legs. I gasped.

"Liked that, did you?" he said, mischievously.

He leaned over and kissed me. I tried to wrap my arms around his neck, but he gently removed them, placing them back on the bed. Still kissing me, he ran one hand back up my arm, and finally placed it on my breast. I arched my back again, pressing myself into his hand. My nipple was rock hard against his palm and I had to break away from his kiss to cry out. He bent down and took my nipple into his mouth, first circling it with his tongue, then sucking it gently.

"Oh, god," I moaned.

Matt stood up and unbuttoned his shirt. I watched as he pulled it off, and then went for the zipper on his jeans. As he undressed, I idly let my finger wander back and forth over my nipple.

"Don't," he said.

I immediately pulled my hand away, raised both my hands and placed them on the bed, on either side of my head--cops and robbers-style.

I immediately pulled my hands away, raised both my hands and placed them on the bed, on either side of my head—cops and robbers-style.

"Yes, sir," I said.

Before pulling off his pants, he reached into his pocket and pulled out a condom.

"I'm clean, Matt. I got tested after Pete. And I'm on the pill. You?"

He dropped the condom and slid onto the bed next to me, wasting no time now in sliding his hand up my body to my breasts. My body responded forcefully.

"I haven't had sex in so long it's not even an issue," he laughed quietly.

Once again, he bent his head to take me in his mouth. His hand traveled downward between my legs, stopping short and resting lightly on my pubic bone.

"What are you doing?" I said. "Touch me."

"Shh…" he said and resumed his course.

I wanted to scream, torn between agony and ecstasy. I had never been more turned on in my life, but I'd also never needed release as much, either. The pleasure verged on pain, and as if sensing the shift, Matt lifted his head kissed his way downwards.

It didn't take long once his tongue touched me for the orgasm to come. It didn't build slowly, but rather came out of nowhere, crashing over me like a tidal wave. I had never come that quickly before. I may have cried out. The aftershocks were still rippling through my body, causing electrical surges that went all the way down to my toes. He kissed the inside of my thigh and pulled himself upwards, until he was positioned directly over me. I reached up and kissed him, pressing myself against him, desperate for maximum contact. He pulled away, taking my lower lip between his teeth and biting lightly. I raised my hips in response, and he reached down to guide himself in.

He moved slowly at first, taking the time to get to know my body and allowing us to establish a rhythm together. He looked into my eyes.

"God, you're beautiful," he whispered.

His speed increased, and he paid close attention to my response, adjusting himself in turn. He was exceptionally good at this; more attentive than any man I'd ever been with.

"Oh, Matt..." I said, totally and utterly under his spell.

I wrapped my legs tightly around his waist as he lowered his head to kiss me. There was nothing I wouldn't have done for him in that moment. I moaned, bucking my hips. He raised himself up from his elbows until his palms were flat against the bed. I felt him move inside me and reached down to rub him, right at the spot where he entered me. He moaned, increasing his speed. I cupped his balls, giving them a slight squeeze, and within moments I felt him contract and shudder as he came.

He collapsed next to me on the bed. We turned our heads to look at each other and started giggling.

"Could you imagine if that had sucked?" he asked.

I laughed.

"That did not suck," I said. "Where the fuck did you learn how to have sex?"

He smiled at me, a devious look in his eye.

"You really want to know?"

"I don't know," I said, suddenly unsure. "Do I?"

He wrapped an arm around me and pulled me up close against him. I snuggled into his chest, tracing the fine hairs that curled up here and there.

"When I was 18, I dated a 23-year-old nymphomaniac," he said. "She used to put me through my paces. I had to read Anaïs Nin for homework. That was the theory. Practice often lasted for hours."

"Well," I murmured. "If you're still in touch, please tell her I say thank you."

He laughed.

"Can you come during intercourse?" he asked.

I was floored. No man had ever asked me that before, not even Josh.

"I haven't yet," I said.

He nodded.

"We can work on that," he said, kissing the top of my head.

I pulled the covers up over us and we drifted off to sleep.

CHAPTER EIGHTEEN

The next morning, I opened my eyes and rolled over in a panic, but there he was, sleeping soundly beside me. I propped myself up on my elbow and watched him. Several minutes went by before he woke, giving me a lazy smile as he rubbed the cobwebs from his eyes.

"Good morning," he murmured.

"Good morning," I said, grinning from ear to ear.

I couldn't help it. There he was, in my bed. I thought about the previous night and felt my face flush.

"I had fun, too," he said, smiling.

I flopped back down on my back and stared

up at the ceiling. He rolled over onto his back and sidled up next to me, so that the lengths of our bodies touched. He took my hand.

"What are you thinking about?" he asked, softly.

"You know exactly what I'm thinking about."

He turned his whole body to face me, and I did the same. He reached over and brushed the hair from my face, tucking it behind my ear. He then traced a line down my jaw to my chin, where he rested his knuckles and used his thumb to stroke my lower lip.

"I don't expect anything of you," he said. "I'm just so fucking grateful for this time we have right now. Let's use it wisely, no?"

I smiled at him, and it was the only signal he needed. He withdrew his hand from my face and placed it on my knee, sliding his hand slowly up my leg. I closed my eyes, taking in a deep breath. I felt his lips, so soft and gentle on my own and tilted my head up eagerly to kiss him. His hand was on my hip, now moving slowly towards my ass. He did this thing with his fingertips that drove me crazy and I could feel the goosebumps rise on my flesh in their wake, leaving me with a delicious hot and cold sensation.

"Open your eyes," he whispered.

His hand cupped my ass and he gave it a slight squeeze before releasing me and continuing his slow journey down the back of my thigh. He held my gaze the entire time, the effect of which was just to make me twice as hot as I already was. He smiled, one side of his mouth pulling up in amusement. He took me by the back of the knee and pulled my leg up over his waist. Anticipating his next move, I closed my eyes and put one hand on his shoulder and the other against his chest.

"Open your eyes," he repeated. "Look at me."

I did as told and stared deep into his eyes. I felt his hand slide between my legs, moving up, slowly, until he…

"Matt," I moaned.

He cupped me with his hand, slowly sliding one finger inside. I held his gaze as my hips started to move against him. He smiled at me, a slow sexy smile that lit me up completely. His hand disappeared, but before I had a chance to stop moving he slid inside me and I arched my back, pressing myself against him.

He went slowly, never breaking his gaze. He slid his hands around and beneath my hips and grabbed my ass, guiding me. He refused to let me speed up, until finally I succumbed and surrendered to his rhythm. Satisfied, he took his left hand off my ass, trailing his fingers over my hips as they made their way between my legs. Using his thumb, he started making slow circles around my clitoris, increasing my desire to speed things up. He gave my ass a light tap.

"No," he said. "Slowly."

"You're so bossy."

"Trust me. Go slowly."

He continued on, refusing to alter his rhythm, and once again I surrendered. He leaned in and kissed me, long and slow. My heart was pounding. I tightened my muscles around him, increasing the friction as much as possible. His thumb never stopped moving, and now increased in speed. I felt the orgasm building, and I broke away from the kiss, staring at him in wonder. He just smiled mischievously and raised his eyebrow, never breaking his own rhythm.

I gripped onto his shoulders as I fell apart around him. Every single part of my body came alive, pulsing and contracting. I may have screamed. It was by far the most earth-shattering orgasm I'd ever had. Somehow, through the fog, I noticed him increase his speed as he worked towards his own finish. I unwrapped my arm from around his neck and put my hand on his ass, digging my nails into him. I pulled him towards me as I picked up his rhythm, wanting to drive him over the edge as he'd done for me.

"Oh, Allie," he whispered.

He held on tight and thrust into me, one last time. I felt his shudder resonate through my body and held him until he stilled. He pulled back and looked at me, smiling.

"See what I did there?" he said, smirking.

"I did see," I said, laughing. "Thank you. That was impressive. Not sure how you pulled that off. I've been trying to do that for years."

Matt just raised his eyebrows and smiled.

I rolled over onto my back and pulled up the covers. I didn't want to get up. I turned my head to look at him.

"Can we just stay in bed until you leave?" I asked.

CHAPTER NINETEEN

Friday flew by as Matt raced to pack and get organized before his flight. I did whatever I could to help, and we took frequent breaks where possible. We couldn't get enough of each other.

That night, we were in my apartment, sitting on the floor of my living room and sharing some Chinese take-out. I had just showered and was in my bathrobe. He was wearing pajama bottoms and a T-shirt. It was close to midnight, but neither of us were prepared to call it a night.

"I wonder if the take-out will be good in Amsterdam," Matt said between mouthfuls.

"Doesn't matter," I said. "Everyone's so high

the food could taste like shit and no one would care."

We both laughed and returned to our food, but I couldn't seem to relax. He was leaving. Tomorrow.

"Penny for your thoughts," he said, nudging my foot with his own.

Fuck it.

"What happens tomorrow?" I asked, point-blank.

He put his chopsticks down in his take-out container and set the whole thing on the coffee table.

"Tomorrow I get on a plane and go to Europe for six months," he said.

"I know that," I said, annoyed. "What happens with us?"

He looked at me and shook his head slowly.

"I don't know," he answered.

I smiled and we sat silently for a while, eating.

"I dated Pete because I was on the rebound."

Matt stopped eating and put down his container. He looked at me, waiting.

"I was with this guy, Josh, for two years. We split up about seven months ago."

"Why?"

I paused. How much did I want to tell him? Fuck it.

"Because we'd been together two years and I wanted to get married. He didn't. I felt he never would, so I left."

Matt was silent for a moment.

"That's really hard, Allie. I'm sorry."

I smiled.

"It's okay. I'm fine now. I actually saw him the other night and, well, it put things into perspective for me. I feel like that door is closed. But for that very same reason, I can't bring myself to offer you anything knowing you're about to take off for six months."

I watched him, trying to see if I could get a sense of what he was thinking. His face was unreadable.

"I understand," he said, finally.

"How about we just take it day by day? No promises, no commitments. You'll be gone six months. That's a long time. We'll text. We'll talk. And we'll see," I said.

He nodded slowly.

"That makes the most sense, I guess," he said.

Matt picked up his food again and watched me eat for a few minutes. He looked sad, and I understood completely. It was so easy, being with him. Even in the middle of a difficult conversation, it hadn't been awkward between us. We'd gotten so close in such a short amount of time, and we just clicked.

He reached over and took the container from my hands and put it down on the table, next to his. He put his hand on my cheek, tracing my bottom lip with his thumb. I melted into his hand and my eyes closed as I savoured the feeling of his touch on my skin, knowing that in mere hours it would be lost to me. I opened my eyes to find him still watching me, but the look in his eyes was slowly changing, from sadness to something very different.

My lips parted as my breathing picked up. The next time his thumb passed over my lip, I took it gently between my teeth, closing my mouth around it. It was his turn to close his eyes. I got on my hands and knees and crawled over to him, climbing into his lap and settling in, so we were face to face. I leaned forward and kissed him, wrapping my arms around his neck. His hands instantly slid into my bathrobe as they snaked around to my back.

"Good Lord, I'm going to miss you," I murmured.

"Our last hurrah," he said, and kissed me again. He gently lifted me off his lap and stood up, putting out his hand to help me up. My robe fell open as I stood, and he just stood there, staring at me and smiling hungrily. He took my hand and led me to the bedroom.

As we crossed the threshold, I slid out of my bathrobe, but held on to the soft belt. I walked over to him and slid my arms around his neck once again, tilting my head up to kiss him. He ran his hands down my naked back, stopping to squeeze my ass. I pressed myself into him, feeling him grow hard through his pajamas.

"You're a naughty girl," he whispered in my ear, giving me a light spank on the rear.

"You have no idea," I whispered back. I took a step back and handed him the belt. "Sometimes, I need to be punished."

His eyes widened slightly, but a slow smile crept across his face and he moved towards me, holding the belt in hand.

"You want me to tie you up?" he asked.

I nodded slowly.

"And you want me to…"

He stared at me, searching my eyes for a clue.

"You could spank me… if you wanted to."

He closed his eyes and opened them, very slowly. He was standing directly in front of me, so close I could smell him, and I closed my eyes and took a deep breath. I opened my eyes, reached up and put my hand on his chest.

"Am I freaking you out?" I asked.

"No," he said. "Is this something you do often?"

"Sometimes. I'm not all BDSM if that's what you're thinking. But sometimes it's nice to relinquish control a little, it turns me on. If you're not comfortable with it…"

"It's not that…" he said.

"Trust me, Matt. I've never done this on a second date before. But you're leaving tomorrow, and I'm really comfortable with you. I thought it would be fun."

He was pulling the belt through his fingers, eyeing me with a look I couldn't quite read. Amusement? Trepidation? Lust?

"Get on the bed," he said.

"Wait— "

"Wait? What about relinquishing control?" he laughed. "I'm trying to do this here."

I laughed in return, realizing he was right.

"You're blushing now?"

"Don't laugh at me," I said.

"Lord, I'm trying. I'm trying. Okay. Get on the bed."

I climbed onto the bed, still laughing and wondering how I'd messed this up so badly. This was about to turn into a slumber party, not hot and heavy sexcapades. I crawled up to the headboard and turned around, lying on my back with my head propped up on the pillows. Matt was still shaking his head, laughing softly to himself.

He pulled the belt apart and took my wrists in hand. He wrapped the belt around them, making sure it wasn't too tight.

"Like this?" he asked.

I nodded.

"Should I tie you to the headboard?"

"That would be fun."

"And I'm supposed to spank you?" he asked.

"If you like."

"Where?"

"Wherever you think might be interesting."

I briefly wondered if he felt like he was back in sex school with his nymphomaniac girlfriend. Hadn't she taught him any of this? At least he was willing – and eager – to learn. So what if he laughed through the whole thing? As long as I got off at some point, it was all good.

By this time, he had finished tying me and securing me to the bedpost. He stood, surveying his work. He eyed me appreciatively.

"That is a pretty fine sight," he said quietly.

I pulled up my knees and parted my legs, inviting him to join me. He groaned softly and pulled off his shirt. I squirmed, and instantly his demeanor changed. He was no longer laughing.

He ran his hand up the curves of my body

while I writhed beneath him. Cupping my breast, he rubbed my nipple between his thumb and forefinger. I moaned, raising my hips off the bed.

"God," he said. "You spring this on me the night before I leave?"

He leaned over, taking my nipple in his mouth, using his tongue to make small circles and then sucking gently. I would've sworn he could make me come like that. He reached down between my legs, lightly stroking me.

"Allie…"

He slid one finger, then two inside. I pushed myself against him, begging him for more speed, more force. He removed his fingers and gave me a little spank, hitting my sweet spot. I let out a cry.

He ran his fingers lightly down my chest, starting at the base of my neck, between my breasts, down to my belly button. He stopped there and gave me a light tap. I raised my hips in response and he smiled. He continued downward, barely skimming across my sex before continuing down the inside of my thigh, where he stopped for another light tap. I moaned again.

"Please," I said. "Just make me come."

"Bo-ring," he said, leaning in and kissing me. He took my head in his hands, roughly pressing his lips against mine. I struggled against the belt, squirming on the bed and his hand returned to its place between my legs.

"Allie, you're so wet..." he murmured against my lips.

"I want you, Matt. Please," I begged. He used his hands to spread my legs apart even further. I closed my eyes and raised my hips, expecting him to take me. Instead, I felt the sharp sting of his flat fingertips against my clitoris. My eyes flew open as I cried out.

"Oh, god... again."

He did it again, smiling down at me, the hunger clear in his eyes. He ran his fingers back up towards by breasts and before I realized what was happening, I felt the sting of his slap against my left nipple, then my right. I lost it then, reason and language left me. I closed my eyes and gave myself over to feeling. My head swam as he returned to his work between my legs, hitting my clitoris, lightly and then sharply, repeatedly until I thought I'd die. I could feel the orgasm building, my body vibrating with every stroke of his hand.

"Matt..."

"I never realized this could be such a turn on."

He pulled off the pajamas. Bracing himself against the bed he positioned himself between my legs, leaning over to take my nipple in his mouth once again. I moaned, twisting against him, unable to wait a second longer. I'd been on the edge since he bound my wrists and if I had to wait one more second…

He slid into me and rode me hard, bracing himself against the bedframe as he thrust repeatedly, driving me over the edge. I exploded around him, crying out and wrapping my legs tightly around his waist, giving myself some kind of anchor as the waves washed over me.

"Oh, god, Allie…"

His entire body seized as he came and then collapsed on top of me. The two of us lay there, and after a few moments he reached up and untied me. I wrapped my arms around him and smiled into his chest. Neither of us made any attempt to move, content to just lie there in each other's arms, enjoying the aftereffects of our orgasms. Just thinking about what we'd just done set me squirming against him, and he laughed.

"I think I might need a little time, hotshot."

CHAPTER TWENTY

The next evening, we stopped by Matt's apartment on the way to the airport to pick up his luggage. Dave had agreed to bring it out, and sure enough he was waiting at the curb for us when we pulled up. Both Matt and I got out of the car and loaded his bags into my trunk. As we worked, Pete came out the front door with his arm around a cute blond – Diana, I suspected. His eyes widened when he saw me.

"What? What are you doing here?" he asked.

Dave stepped in between us and Pete and put a hand on his shoulder and nodded towards Diana. Pete took the hint.

"Allie and Matt met up a few days ago and have been spending some time together," Dave said. "You should introduce Diana to Allie."

Pete cleared his throat, and leading Diana by the hand walked up to me.

"Allie, this is Diana, my girlfriend," he said, not looking me in the eye.

I put out my hand and shook Diana's warmly.

"It's a pleasure to meet you," I said.

"Likewise," Diana replied.

"Matt, dude, I just wanted to come out and say goodbye," Pete said. "Have a great trip. We'll take care of your shit here."

Matt clapped Pete on the shoulder and smiled.

"Thanks, Pete. I'll be in touch about my mail and stuff," he said.

Matt and Dave exchanged a quick hug, we got into the car, and we were off. I turned on the radio, assuming neither of us were in the mindset for conversation.

"That was fun last night," Matt said.

I smiled, remembering all too clearly.

"It was," I murmured.

I shifted in my seat.

"I'm still thinking about—"

"Different topic, please. I'd like to get you to the airport in one piece," I said.

A few moments later we pulled up to the departure terminal at the airport. I'd already decided not to go in with him. It would be too hard. We pulled into an unloading zone and got out of the car. We said nothing as we pulled out his luggage, and I waited while he went to retrieve a cart.

When he got back, he stood before me, looking into my eyes. He reached out his hand, cupping my chin.

"This sucks," he said.

"I know," I said. "But let's just see what happens. Text me when you land so I know you're okay."

I leaned up, winding my arms around his neck and pulling him down towards me. I kissed him, closing my eyes as I savoured those last few minutes, the feel of his lips on mine. He wrapped his arms around my waist, drawing me in even closer and returning the kiss, with considerably more passion.

"Sure you don't want to come in?" he asked, an evil glint in his eye.

I laughed and pulled away from the embrace.

"Positive," I said.

I gave him a smile, touched his cheek and turned to get into the car. There was really nothing to say. We'd known each other so little time. I stood at the driver's side door, watching him wheel his luggage cart into the terminal.

He stopped at the door and turned to wave. I waved back, got into the car, and drove away.

CHAPTER TWENTY-ONE

Weeks passed and the weather got cooler as September morphed into October. Matt and I sexted every night, and I had zero desire to go out and meet people. I looked forward to those moments together, even though we were so far apart. And the time difference didn't help much.

One night, after a particular steamy exchange, I was having trouble sleeping and having given up, got out of bed and ambled into the kitchen. I pulled out my trusty box and twisted up a joint. I sat down at the kitchen table to smoke it, idly hitting the keys on my laptop as I did so. It was a little past midnight. I remembered the last time Matt and I were in this kitchen together. It was the morning he'd left for Europe. I'd gotten up early to make him breakfast – homemade waffles with whipped cream and strawberry coulis.

Inspired, I put the joint down in the ashtray and fired up my laptop. I thought maybe I'd write up a quick story about that morning and send it to Matt, give him some... material. I smiled at the thought and got to work.

I woke up early, wanting to make him breakfast before he left for the airport. Six months was a long time to be gone, especially when we'd had so little time together. I stood in the kitchen, dressed in his T-shirt and a hair tie. I threw together some waffle batter and pulled out the strawberry coulis that I'd made the day before from the fridge. I dripped some on my finger from the squirt bottle and put my it to my lips, tasting to make sure it was perfect. It was. I was busy whipping the cream when I heard a noise behind me. I turned, and there he was, standing in his boxer briefs and nothing else. I smiled.

"What are you doing?" he asked.

"Making you breakfast," I said, smiling demurely. I gave the cream a final whip, licking the whisk slowly before putting it in the sink. He walked over to me, took my hand, picked up the bowl and said, "Come."

I smiled to myself and grabbed the coulis as I

stumbled over my feet on the way out of the kitchen. Within moments we were in bed, using our bodies as canvases and creating masterpieces in red and white. We laughed, enjoying a lighthearted moment. And then he leaned over and gently licked a drop of coulis that was running off my nipple. I breathed in sharply as he reached out, cupping the bottom of breast and taking me into his mouth, sucking, nibbling. I moaned, wrapping my hands around his head and pulling him in closer.

The next time I looked up at the clock it was 4 a.m. I'd written two thousand words and they were *hot*. I finished off the forgotten joint in the ashtray and went to bed.

In the morning, I read over the piece I'd written the night before. It was good. Really good. I sat for a moment, staring out the kitchen window while I considered my options. Matt would love it. Or would he freak out? Should I even send it to him? I was seconding guessing myself, but objectively, I knew it was good writing. My index finger tapped on the keyboard while I sat and thought it through. Finally, after who knows how long, I hit the print button. I collected the sheets from the printer, folded them up and stuffed them in my purse.

*

I had a few meetings that morning at the office, so I set up a lunch with Lynn at 1 p.m. My meetings ended early, and I took the opportunity to corner Sarah, my editor.

"Got a minute?" I asked her.

"For you? Sure," she said.

She turned and led the way into her office. Once inside, she shut the door and we both took a seat, her behind the desk, me on the couch along the wall.

"What's up?" she asked.

"I was wondering if you'd take a look at something for me."

I pulled the folded pages from my bag. I stood and hesitated for a fraction of a second before leaning over and handing them to her. She took them, a curious look on her face.

"Now?" she asked.

I shrugged. Sarah looked down and her eyes skimmed the first few lines. She looked up at me, an amused look on her face, and then settled back into her chair, bringing the pages closer to her face. She took her time, reading slowly. I sat there, nervous as hell. What had I been thinking? She's my food editor. When she finished, she folded the pages up carefully and put them on her desk.

"Allie," she said. I said nothing. "Allie, this is

really good."

All the nervous tension drained from my body and I broke out into a ridiculous grin.

"You think so?" I asked.

"Yes. I really do," she said. "There's nothing I can do with it, but I know someone who can. Let me put you in touch."

"Thank you, Sarah. Seriously," I said.

"You're not planning to leave me, are you? Start an erotica writing career? You're a great food critic, Allie," she said.

"I'm not going anywhere," I promised.

Sarah smiled.

"Phew. I'll get you that contact info and email it later. In the meanwhile," she said, smiling mischievously, "can I keep this?"

She held up the pages. I laughed.

"Sure. Knock yourself out," I said, and walked out the door.

CHAPTER TWENTY-TWO

"I love Mexican food," Lynn gushed, poring over her menu.

We were seated at a two-top in the window at a newly-opened taqueria in the heart of the financial district. It was an odd location, but I'd heard the food was fantastic.

"You just love the margaritas," I said, laughing.

The waiter came over and took our orders. I was tempted to order everything on the menu – I actually did love Mexican food – but I showed some restraint, and between us we ordered six appetizers and five mains. Once again, the waiter looked at us like we were nuts.

"So, how's everything?" Lynn asked. "You lonely?"

"I don't know," I said, shrugging. "I miss the sex. I miss him. But we barely knew each other. It's weird. It doesn't feel like it was rebound sex."

"Because it wasn't," Lynn said. "He was not your rebound guy."

We both grew silent as I considered the implications of this statement.

"Still sexting?" she asked, eyeing me shrewdly.

"Yes," I said, blushing. "Almost every night."

Lynn shook her head.

"Have you thought about an impromptu vacation?"

I stopped. I hadn't. In fact, the idea hadn't even crossed my mind. A trip to Amsterdam. *Why not?*

"I don't know, Lynn... you don't think that's a bit much? Like I said, we hardly know each other..."

"Come on, Allie. You two connected. There was chemistry from across the room with you guys. Even I felt it. I'm sure he'd be thrilled. You go for a week. That's nothing. Doesn't work out, you travel around a bit and come home."

She made it sound so reasonable. *Why not?*

Later, I bumped into Trish while getting the mail.

"Hey, how's it going?" I asked her.

"Ugh," she said, shaking her head. "Living with the rents is starting to drive me nuts. I've got to find a place."

I glanced up from my mail and studied her for a moment. *Why not?*

"Listen, Trish. I'm thinking about going to Amsterdam next week, for about a week. Would you want to stay at my place and watch Loki for me? I'd be happy to pay you."

"Pay me? Are you crazy? I'd love to stay at your place! With Loki! OMG, Allie! You're the best!" she screamed.

She launched herself at me and gave me a big bear hug. I couldn't help but smile. As I climbed the stairs, I was already mentally going through a packing checklist.

That evening, after I'd eaten and was relaxing on the couch, I opened my laptop and started researching flights to Amsterdam. There was one leaving on Saturday at a great price – a last-minute discount. Three days away. Was I really going to do this?

I heard the familiar ping and immediately checked my mail. There was one from Sarah, passing along that contact info. Tara Sheen. I'd never heard the name, but then again, I hadn't really worked with any editors in this area before. I opened a blank email and sent her a pitch, attaching a copy of the story I'd already written. My heart skipped a beat as I hit send, but hey – it didn't hurt to try. What was the worst that could happen?

They could publish it.

Suddenly, that thought was more terrifying than anything else. I decided then and there I needed a pen name. I pulled out a pad and pen and got to work brainstorming. And then it hit me – I had to tell Sarah I was going away. *Shit.*

Deciding I'd go in and speak to her in the morning, I climbed into bed and turned on the TV.

CHAPTER TWENTY-THREE

"Amsterdam?" Sarah said, an amused smile on her lips.

"Yes," I said. "I have a friend who's there on a six-month contract and I figured I'd pay a visit," I said.

She nodded slowly, studying my face. Her eyes lit up.

"Want to write it off?" she asked.

I sat up, interested.

"What did you have in mind?"

"Why don't you do a tour of local Dutch cuisine? I think that could be a lot of fun."

"Will you cover any expenses?"

"You're good," Sarah laughed. "Tell you what. I'll cover three nights in a hotel."

I paused.

"I don't think I'll need a hotel," I said, blushing.

"Ahhh, *that* kind of friend," Sarah said. "Okay. Half your flight. And the food, of course."

"Deal," I said. I stood up to leave.

"When do you go?"

"Saturday," I said, deciding then and there I was really going to do this.

"Have a great trip," she said, smiling.

As I was heading to the elevator, my phone rang. I looked at the screen but didn't recognize the number.

"Hello?" I said.

"Is this Allie Styles?" a woman's voice said.

"Yes," I said. "Who's this?"

"This is Tara Sheen."

Holy shit.

"Ms. Sheen. Thank you so much for calling. I'm surprised to hear from you so quickly," I said.

"I don't beat around the bush, Ms. Styles," she said, coolly. "You are an exceptionally talented writer. Why have I never heard your name before?"

I take a seat on one of the plush armchairs in the reception area and look around to ensure no one is within earshot.

"Because this is my first foray," I said, nervously.

"This is your first piece of erotica?" she asked, the incredulity evident in her voice.

"Yes?" I whispered, barely audible. I feared this woman.

"Can you write more?" she asked, all business once again.

"Yes," I said.

"A lot more?" she asked.

Holy crap.

"Yes," I said firmly.

"Good," she said.

She proceeded to lay out a deal that would involve me delivering two thousand words a week, and her providing me with enough money that I could take off to Amsterdam for some quick sexcapades. I thought I was going to faint.

"Can you tell me a little about where the work will be published?" I asked.

"We have a website we started a few months back. We're slowly building traffic. We specialize in high end erotica writing and photography. I think your work would be a perfect fit. Do we have a deal?"

"Yes," I said, stunned.

"Good. I'll expect your next piece in my inbox on Monday morning. Have a pleasant day," she said, and hung up.

I rode the elevator down to the lobby in a state of shock. I walked out the front door and it's possible that I floated home. I was going to be earning money writing erotica. And there I'd been, looking for a side hustle. A SIDE HUSTLE! Ha! This could turn into a full-time gig. I whipped out my phone and called Lynn, practically screaming into the phone.

I had two days to get ready for my trip. I couldn't stop thinking about the look on Matt's face when I walked through the door. I couldn't wait to see it. We continued to text, and sext, and I never once let on that within days we would be together, touching each other, taking each other to incredible places.

*

I spent the flight writing my next story. I wrote about the first time we had sex, how he touched every part of my body, teasing me, making me wait, until finally bringing me to an earth-shattering orgasm. It was probably a mistake, given the amount of squirming I was doing in my seat. The man next to me kept glancing over, giving me funny looks. *Go ahead, sucker, this is money in my pocket.* I smiled to myself.

We landed early the next morning, and I had managed to get a few hours of sleep before arriving at Schiphol. After deplaning and clearing security, I headed straight for the bathrooms to freshen myself up. No way I was going to see Matt after six weeks looking like I'd just spent the night traveling. Even though I had. I washed my face, brushed my teeth, re-applied my makeup and put on some deodorant. I tried desperately to do something with my hair, but in the end I just put it up.

I was in the cab on the way to his place when I remembered to turn my cell phone back on. There was a buzz, and a text came in. From Matt.

Hey.

Hey, yourself.

Where are you?

I checked the time and did the mental math. It was 10 a.m. Amsterdam time.

It's 4 a.m. I'm in bed. Where do you think I am? Where are you?

I had a sudden panic that maybe he wasn't at home. Oh, well. I could wait.

I'm in bed.

A slow smile spread across my face. I'm coming, Matt…

So late? Aren't you an early riser?

I just had the most erotic dream about you.

I glanced uncomfortably at the cab driver and shifted in my seat.

I have those all the time. Tell me more.

What are wearing right now? I want you naked for this.

The car pulled over. I leaned forward.

"Where are we?" I asked.

"Just at the corner of where you want to be. The address is right there," the cab driver said, pointing towards a small, narrow house sandwiched between a row of other small, narrow houses, each of them painted a different colour.

It was a beautiful street, right along the canal. I paid the driver, got out and grabbed my bag. *Shit, Matt!*

Allie? You there.

I'm here. Just doing what you asked.

I smiled to myself, thinking in just a few minutes, I'd be doing it live. I stopped outside the door, double-checked the address, and climbed up the long narrow flight of stairs. It was pretty scary. Thankfully, there was a decent-sized landing at the door, and I knocked, waiting for him to answer. I couldn't wait to see the shock on his face. I frantically dropped my bag and undid my top button as I heard footsteps approach. This was hands down the best decision I'd ever made in my life. This was going to be mind-blowing, off-the-charts sex. My body ached just thinking about it.

The door swung open, and there stood a tall, leggy blond dressed in nothing but an oversized white V-neck T-shirt and a pair of white panties. She was gorgeous, and her nipples were rock hard, poking at her shirt like they were desperate to escape. I stood there and just stared at her.

She smiled at me and cocked her head.

"Can I help you," she asked, in an accent I couldn't quite place.

"I… I was looking for my friend, but I think I've got the wrong…" I stuttered, shocked.

I picked up my bag and backed away, bracing myself for the treacherous descent down those stairs. She smiled and nodded her head.

"Matt, honey?" she called. "I think someone's here to see you."

In the background, I saw a bedroom door open and out came Matt, wearing nothing but his pajama bottoms. I felt like I'd been punched in the stomach. I couldn't breathe. I grabbed onto the doorframe and my eyes widened as I saw Matt moving towards me.

You are a strong woman, Allie Styles. Don't you let this asshole get to you.

And that's the last thing I remember before I passed out.

*

Dying to know what happens next? Read an excerpt from *Deception*, the next book in the series:

It was a beautiful Sunday morning in October as I stood outside my boutique hotel in Amsterdam, contemplating the building. Boutique might have been generous – the place was incredibly narrow and had to have been tiny inside. I looked back, but my cab driver was already gone. I took a deep breath and walked through the front door.

There was no lobby, just a long desk by a narrow staircase. A sign over the desk read RECEPTION, and underneath, in smaller print, *No joints before lunch*. I rolled my eyes. Gotta love Amsterdam. I rang the bell on the desk and a short, curly-haired woman in what can only be described as a frock emerged from a door I hadn't even noticed. She looked at me and gave me a funny smile.

"Ms. Styles," she said with a thick Dutch accent.

"Yes."

I proceeded to check in, grabbed my bag, and climbed the stairs. I'd never been to Amsterdam before, but I was beginning to suspect there would be a lot of stairs involved. On the third floor, I put my key in the lock of the only door and turned the knob, but was met with resistance when I tried to push it open.

Looking in, I saw the bed blocking my way. The room was tiny. I squeezed in, dropped my bags on the one chair, and looked around. White walls, one small painting of a tree, a single bed, a chair, and a door. *Please let that lead to a bathroom.* I walked over and slid the door open. Sure enough, it was a minuscule bathroom with a sink, a toilet, a showerhead over the toilet, and a drain in the floor.

"Oh, good Lord."

I walked into the bathroom and looked in the mirror. At 31, I still looked like I was in my mid-twenties. I never knew if that was a good thing or not. Brown curly hair, a small smattering of freckles across my nose, and my too-big mouth, or at least I had always thought so. One guy had once referred to my mouth as generous. It left me with the weirdest feeling.

I washed my face quickly and changed into a fresh T-shirt and cardigan. I fixed my hair as best I could and walked out the door. I was jetlagged as hell, but if I slept then, I'd be ruined for days. Best if I stayed awake until at least dinner.

I grabbed a walking map of the city off the front desk as I headed out the door. I had no intention of doing any real sight-seeing—I was way too tired for that. But I had to walk around the city or I'd spend the entire day rehashing the morning's events.

I'd flown across the ocean to surprise Matt with a week of wild sex, only to have him surprise me by having another woman answer the door. In her underwear. He had *just* been sexting with me. The shock, combined with the jet lag, was too much and I just passed out. Right at the front door, right in front of them.

When I came to, I was on a couch, with both Matt and the leggy blond standing over me, peering anxiously into my eyes. I jumped up.

"I'm sorry," I said. "This was a mistake."
***

Other books by Sydney Campbell:

Allie Styles Romance Series:
Temptation (Book 1)
Deception (Book 2)
Reckonings (Book 3)
Beginnings (Book 4)

Courtyard Tales of Contemporary Romance
Reawakening
Redemption
Reckless